The *Gauntlet's* motion was violent but she was competing; then suddenly she seemed to get out of phase with the wave-lengths. There was a shuddering jar up forward as if she had hit something solid; her bow, instead of lifting at the bottom of the wave-trough, continued to drive downwards. To Tommy on the bridge it seemed that she had decided to dive, and he wondered momentarily if the vents had been opened and if the submarine was about to take her last plunge; then he heard Morgan Jones' voice, shrill and desperate: 'Look out, sir, it's coming!' He looked ahead and saw for a moment a towering wave crest coming from right above him, dozens of feet over the bridge. It foamed, it hissed, and then it struck the bridge and engulfed it, plucking with mighty hands at the two men who hung on there, against the solid wall of sea . . .

Also by Gilbert Hackforth-Jones

CHINESE POISON
THE STERN CHASE
ONE MAN'S WARS
SECURITY RISK
ALL STATIONS TO MALTA
YELLOW PERIL

and published by Corgi Books

Gilbert Hackforth-Jones

Dangerous Trade

CORGI BOOKS
A DIVISION OF TRANSWORLD PUBLISHERS LTD
A NATIONAL GENERAL COMPANY

DANGEROUS TRADE
A CORGI BOOK 0 552 09383 1

Originally published in Great Britain by
Hodder & Stoughton Ltd.

PRINTING HISTORY
Hodder & Stoughton edition published 1952
Hodder & Stoughton edition reprinted 1952
Hodder & Stoughton edition reprinted 1952
Hodder & Stoughton edition reprinted 1955
Corgi edition published 1957
Corgi edition reissued 1973

This book is set in Intertype Baskerville

Corgi Books are published by Transworld Publishers Ltd.,
Cavendish House, 57-59 Uxbridge Road,
Ealing, London, W.5.
Made and printed in Great Britain by
Hunt Barnard Printing Ltd., Aylesbury, Bucks.

NOTE: The Australian price appearing on the back cover is the recommended retail price.

DEDICATION

Once a year the Submarine Branch of the Royal Navy holds its annual reunion of submarine officers. It is heavily attended by 'submariners' past and present, and has been going on for the past half-century. At these gatherings we meet all the officer-friends we ever had in submarines and occasionally an old enemy. The years drop away; time means nothing; the Sub-Lieutenant of fifty-one talks reverently to the Lieutenant of sixty-four and is called 'sir' by the Admiral of forty-nine. One talks and talks, and occasionally listens, until at a chosen moment the Admiral Commanding Submarines speaks.

He bids us welcome, and tells us how things have gone in the past year. He speaks of grievous losses, of hopes for the future, of the passing of old-timers, and of the recruiting of the young. He bids us come again; and this we do, for we never seem to see everybody with whom we would have liked to talk until just before it is time to go home.

This story, part truth and part fiction, is dedicated to the new 'submariners', as a small token of our admiration at the way in which they have adjusted themselves to the complications of modern machinery, without losing the human touch, which still makes the submarines reunion the best cocktail party this side of the Styx.

Those who had a hand in the events narrated above will not need to be told that the characterisation in this book is entirely fictional, and is not intended, in any way, to represent any living person.

G. H-J.

CHAPTER ONE

A GREY sky; a sullen sea which merged into an indeterminate horizon; a hot moisture-laden wind, which brought no relief on that sultry afternoon, somewhere near Ceylon. Nothing very pleasant about anything, reflected Morgan Jones, the navigator of H.M. Submarine *Gauntlet*, and having thus reflected, he burst into song, for he was a Welshman and always sang for the purpose of indicating a state of misery.

The two 'look-outs' on the bridge beside him looked at each other and lifted their heads to indicate that it was their bad luck to have to listen yet again, to the navigator's limited repertoire. Silently, one of them passed the other a cigarette, they shared a match and resumed their vigil; for it was war time and even the leaden Indian Ocean could conceal a lurking Jap submarine. It would be a great pity for the *Gauntlet*, which had survived the last dangerous period in the Mediterranean, to go now; if the officers and crew had anything to do with it, they would certainly continue to survive. 'No unnecessary hostages to fortune,' was their unwritten law. They were punctilious in watch-keeping, and in the care and maintenance of their vessel. The war was coming to an end, they had achieved much; all the more reason, therefore, to try and survive to reap the fruits of their labours; and now, here they were speeding towards their destination, Trincomalee, to join up with the *Nth* Flotilla for the last stages of the war.

'What e'er befall –
I shall recall –
That sunlit mountain side,'

carolled the navigator; then he caught sight of the Captain's head and shoulders emerging from the conning-tower hatchway and the song died on his lips. In a few seconds the Captain was standing beside him sweeping the horizon with his glasses as a matter of routine more than anything else.

'All right, Pilot,' he said in a mild voice, 'I'll hold the fort till the Sub comes up – he's gone for the hot roly-poly in rather a big way.'

'Thank you, sir,' said Morgan Jones, 'course three hundred and fifty-nine, three hundred revolutions, nothing in sight. The noon position is on the chart.' He dropped down the conning-tower hatch with the speed of a hungry man going in search of food, and was soon sitting at the table in his shirt sleeves.

'Bully beef and potato pie and hot roly-poly,' the First-Lieutenant was saying – 'a nice seasonable dish, Chief, but don't you think it's a trifle warming for this climate?'

Mr Miles shook his head. 'The warmer the day the hotter the food should be,' he said, 'as long as I'm mess caterer that's how it'll be and you know it, Number One. Anyway, there's nothin' else to have, whether you know it or not.'

'Good old Chiefy,' said Jones helping himself liberally to a solid mass of pie, 'not only does he provide unsuitable food, but he pretends it's good for us.'

'So it is,' said Mr Miles, 'it's all a matter of calories. Look at what the black people eat here. Hot curry. That proves my point.'

'Doesn't prove anything,' said Number One, 'curry came in to hide the smell of rotten meat, before refrigerators were invented, that's all. Anyway, why roly-poly pudding? Couldn't we have had some bottled fruit?'

'I'm keeping the fruit for our first patrol out here,' said the Chief.

'Jolly good pie all the same,' said the Navigator, with his mouth full. 'What are you waiting for, Gannet?'

The Sub, whose appetite had earned him the familiar soubriquet grinned. 'I was waiting to see whether you'd leave any pudding,' he confessed. 'I'm rather fond of jam roll.'

Mr Miles clicked his tongue.

'Eat the 'orse and chase the rider,' he said, as if it were an original statement. 'That's what 'e'd do, Number One, wouldn't he, eat the 'orse and chase the rider.'

'We'd better get the cox'n to give him a worm-powder,' said Number One, coarsely.

'Just because I've a healthy appetite!' complained the Sub.

'Healthy,' said Mr Miles. 'It can't be healthy to eat as

much as what you do – stands to reason.' He got up and reached for his pipe and baccy.

'Have a heart, Chief – don't smoke till I've finished eating – you've no idea what it pongs like.'

'Some people,' said the Chief, 'don't know good tobacco when they smells it.' He went aft to his beloved engines before anyone could think of a suitable rejoinder.

The *Gauntlet*'s wardroom was placed just forward of the control-room. It was a small box-like compartment with built-in bunks, chests of drawers, a settee and a table. Folding camp-stools and a bookcase completed the furnishings and the room itself could be screened from the gangway which gave access to the forward part of the submarine, by a heavy rep curtain. In the temperature prevailing it was never pulled, for the officers preferred the constant traffic of men, backwards and forwards, to the stuffiness which privacy would have entailed. The total size of the wardroom was about half that of a small caravan and in this little box the officers managed to live for periods up to two months at a time. The cooking arrangements were slightly farther forward and consisted of an urn, an oven and a hot-plate. The cook, Able Seaman Bert Davis, known as ever as the 'Wardroom flunkey', managed to turn out large quantities of plain but palatable food and made very little fuss about it. Normally, when the submarine was on patrol, the cooking did not take place until after dark, when she was once more on the surface, for during diving hours the temperature was such as to discourage any idea of hot food; moreover it was advisable not to expend any more electricity than was absolutely necessary. On this long passage from Alexandria to Trincomalee, however, something like peace-time routine was being observed. The submarine remained for the most part on the surface, diving for half an hour twice daily to exercise the crew, and was proceeding for the rest of the time at a speed of ten knots towards her destination. Meal times were adjusted to this placid existence, compared to which the hot and humid conditions of fourteen-hour days beneath the surface was purgatory itself.

On this day, the last before their arrival at their destination, there was a general feeling that they had been travelling for a very long time, as indeed they had. They were thoroughly accustomed to the steady purposeful rhythm of the engines, the high temperature had ceased to be remarkable and they were all in that peculiar state of mind which comes to travellers who have been together through a long journey; a great reluctance to have the rhythm broken. The thought of arriving at this new submarine base, under an unknown flotilla Captain, and going off on operations against the Japanese presented no welcome picture. If they had to spend their war at sea in submarines how better than to travel hopefully for ever?

Forward of the wardroom lived the Petty Officers, six in number, who were entitled by rank to mess apart. Theirs was an even smaller compartment than the officers' but the use of folding cots for sleeping gave them more room in proportion. A long table, flanked by large box settees, was the sole furnishing of this mess, apart from a small mirror, and a number of photographs of film stars. The senior member of the mess and, in fact, the senior rating of the *Gauntlet* was Chief Petty Officer Hinton, a large man, well endowed with all carnal desires. Known throughout the branch as 'Guts', because of his corporation, he ruled the submarine with a benevolent despotism which was as inconsistent as it was effective. He always won his battles, and there were many, for he possessed the traditional feeling of superiority over the engine-room branch, the senior members of which were all of chief-petty-officer status. Only by virtue of his being the disciplinary head of the ship was 'Guts' Hinton made an Acting Chief Petty Officer but he never ceased to impress his status upon the inhabitants of the Engine-Room Artificers' Mess. As cox'n of the submarine, moreover, he acted as ship's steward and was in charge of the numerous submarine 'comforts' in the form of bottled fruits and other delicacies which are provided to supplement the service rations. These, and the rum ration gave 'Guts' Hinton a great deal of power, for he was able to increase, or withhold, his daily issue according to the terms on which he was with the individual members of the crew. If he thought a man had done conspicuously well there was always a second tot of rum for him, neat; if, however, he was displeased with him the first and only tot was already watered. 'Guts' had a masterful personality and his misuse of the English language was a lasting delight both to officers and crew. His despotic ways, though resented by many, were recognised as unchangeable, and nobody, even in their most bitter moods of resentment, thought of stating a complaint to the officers.

Hinton's assistant, or second coxswain, was as might well be expected, a mild mannered chap whose favourite expression was 'O.K. 'swain'. He was a pleasant, good-looking young Petty Officer with whom it was impossible to quarrel. He did his work well enough but only just. His name was George Badger.

Bert Toogood was the Petty Officer Telegraphist, a 'hostilities only' rating who had volunteered for service in submarines and had risen to Petty Officer in under a year. Because of this and because he was not a long-service man, Hinton did his best to squash Toogood in every possible way.

The other members of the mess were Jo Parker, the Torpedo Gunner's mate, a worthy married type who was always wiping the stains of 'Torpoil' off his long hands with a piece of waste, looking as he did so, very like Lady Macbeth under different circumstances: Tom Gurney, Chief Stoker, and his assistant Fortescue, whose christian name never emerged, but who was invariably called Clarence because of his slightly patrician surname. 'Arry Leeton, Petty Officer and in charge of the electrics, completed the mess.

On the other side of an eighth-of-an-inch plywood bulkhead lived the Artificers, in awful and solitary splendour, under the suzerainty of the Chief, Izzy Sammons, a tough little east-end Jew, who had strayed into the engineering profession as the result of an abortive love-affair in Bermondsey, and having served his apprenticeship, had risen rapidly to Chief, because his native ability and wit made him an outstanding personality. It also made him a natural enemy for a man like the coxwain, and it speaks volumes for the good sense of Mr Miles that he was able to prevent the racial enmity of the two men from causing a major upheaval. The Chief E.R.A.'s three assistants were decent, if colourless, technicians who, like so many ordinary fellows, just go on with their jobs and kept their thoughts to themselves. With them messed the Electrical Artificer, Weremouth, a well-spoken, well educated youngster who should have been commissioned, but whose deceptively mild manner had resulted in his rejection by a selection board who were not accustomed to looking beneath the surface of either things, or people.

The seamen of the submarine messed together with the Telegraphists and Signal ratings in the fore crew space. There were sixteen altogether and because they were able to overflow into the torpedo space forward they had more room than anybody else aboard; while the ten stokers, who lived right aft on top of the propellers, and near the great electric main motors, had by far the worst of it. Apart from the noise, the vibration and the extreme heat, they were cut off from the outer world by the clattering engine-room, and could never have the faintest idea what was going on. Yet, they were a contented lot, who seemed to be completely oblivious of the appalling conditions under which they existed for months at a time. The engine-room of a submarine is a draughty, noisy affair, the stokers' mess-deck had a maximum headroom of just over five feet, yet the volunteers continued to pour in to the submarine branch and the standard of health remained exceedingly high. It seems that if you *feed* and *lead* men well they can endure the most extraordinary conditions of life. Of food we have already made mention; of leadership as yet we have not, so let us now climb the vertical ladder from the control-room, through the conning-tower, up to the bridge and take a good look at Lieutenant Tommy Woodstock, D.S.O., D.S.C., Royal Navy.

With all those letters after his name there ought to have been more distinction about Tommy's bearing; but here was no lantern-jawed hero. At first sight this small man in khaki shirt and shorts, wrinkled stockings and soft shoes, and wearing a solar topee of doubtful colour, looked rather like a solemn young scoutmaster. He spoke in a mild voice, his manner was faintly apologetic, and under stress of difficulty and danger he was even more subdued. He seldom raised his voice; when things got difficult he became as silent as it was practicable to be. He had commanded the *Gauntlet* for over a year now, and his crew had remained with him without more than a few changes due to sickness and promotion. Bill Brown, the First-Lieutenant, frankly worshipped him, and was dreading the day when this partnership would be broken, while Morgan Jones and the Gannet also adored their Captain. As for Mr Miles, the Warrant Engineer, he reckoned that Tommy Woodstock would probably keep him alive, and as a married man that was his main preoccupation; that is not to say that Mr Miles was not a superlatively good engineer. He was, but he was also a realist, and fond of life.

It is customary to describe heroes as being completely oblivious of the affection and respect which they engender in their followers. There may be such people who walk through life on a different plane to their fellow-creatures, but we have never met them. Tommy, with all his mildness of manner, was fully aware of his hold upon his ship's company. He did nothing that was not deliberate, and he was also aware of his own personal deficiencies. For one thing, he was convinced that he was a lazy man. Someone had told him he was lazy many years before; this statement now acted as a perpetual hair-shirt to Tommy. If people were lazy in this war they wouldn't help to win it, and if they were in submarines they wouldn't live to see it won.

It is usual when writing about a leader of fighting men to ascribe much higher motives to him than he actually possesses and, by the time he had been dead a hundred years a simple man, who simply did his best, is vested with a spirit of patriotism, which, if he had possessed it, would have made him a better statesman than fighter.

The sole reason for Tommy's devotion to duty was no more than a desire to do what he had been told to do as well as he could do it, and, if possible, to survive to tell the tale, and to live with his pretty young wife who now was busily striving to be a good Wren, so as to take her mind off the dreadful and distinct possibility of waking up to find herself a submarine officer's widow.

The love of Audrey and Tommy Woodstock had been a simple and clean affair. Tommy on a month's survivors' leave, after he'd had what is professionally know as a 'swim', after Dunkirk, had volunteered for submarines and had fallen in love simultaneously. Their total married life together since nineteen forty did not add up to more than a few months. They wrote daily to each other and debated fiercely whether it would be better to get on with having a baby, 'just in case', but somehow they had never reached a decision and now Tommy was going to be stationed in Ceylon, while Audrey was pulling every possible string to get herself drafted there as well. It has often been suggested, especially by the older generation of shell-backs, that marriage by junior officers, who are on hazardous service, is likely to blunt the fine edge of their determination. There seems to be no justification for this statement; most of the world's heroes were married men; certainly, the only effect that marriage had had upon Tommy was to quicken his desire to get the war over so that he could see more of his wife. It was this motive, plus the feeling that he must be careful not to be lazy, that had driven him along to achieve the glory which was already his when this story opens, and resulted in the happenings which are chronicled below.

CHAPTER TWO

'FINISHED with the engines.' With this utterance Tommy laid his burden of responsibility down and was free to look around him at the new world to which he had brought his command.

The *Gauntlet* was now lying neatly square with three other vessels of the same class alongside the towering sides of the old depot-ship *Carpentaria.* Her crew, whilst ostensibly squaring off on deck, were busily exchanging gossip with the men who had crowded over to the nearest submarine and were recognising old friends. On the boat-deck of the depot-ship were gathered a knot of officers, looking at the new addition to the flotilla for lack of anything better to do. Tommy recognised a friend, gave a cheerful wave and went below to dress himself in suitable apparel for reporting to the captain of the flotilla; *Captain S/M,* as he was called.

Then, with a handful of personal letters, he went forward through the submarine, up the fore-hatch, open for the first time for three weeks, on to the forecasing, where a gang-plank was at that moment ready for him to cross to the next vessel. The men on the upper deck stood still, as the little white-clad figure of the man who had led them so far, and would lead them to the end in store for them, walked nimbly across the springy plank; then they lit cigarettes and abandoned all further pretence of work.

At the depot-ship's gangway stood a reception committee, all very pukka, and the thin wail of a bosun's 'Call' indicated that the Commanding Officer of the *Gauntlet* was being piped over the side, as was his right when making a ceremonial call. He stood at the top of the gangway for a moment with his arm at the salute and then took the proffered hand of the Commander, an ageing repaint with a pleasant smile.

'Woodstock? Used to know your father very well, you're

not at all like him. Pity he went in that E boat.' That was the Submarine Branch all over, you didn't join a new flotilla in the sense that you joined a new ship. Everybody knew everybody in that outfit, and this old type had been a contemporary of his father, who had been lost in that other war. Tommy couldn't remember him except as a voice and a large tweed coat smelling of masculine things, but Commander Wardle had known him as well as Tommy knew 'Shiner' Wright, who was standing at the back of the reception committee grinning like a rat-trap. This, thought Tommy, isn't so bad. Much of the foreboding which had assailed him all the way from Egypt seemed to have been swept away. The natives were definitely friendly.

'Wotcher, Tommy,' said Shiner, punching him in the midriff. 'How are you?'

'Fine,' said Tommy, looking round him for other faces, in particular that of George Carter who had been his 'raggy' in the Med. Something in his inquiring glance brought a sudden change of temperature in the little group; it was hardly necessary to say anything, but something had to be said.

'The *Gordian,*' said Shiner, 'we heard yesterday. Stinking luck.'

There was a silence.

'Poor old George,' said Tommy and left it at that. The foreboding had been justified. This was a bloody business and it always seemed to pick the good chaps. George Carter had been one in a million. Had been – a few letters to write to the next-of-kin – a packing up of personal effects, the painting-out of the name *Gordian* on the staff office information board and the substitution of another name – the *Gauntlet.* He shivered for a moment. A voice in his ear; Commander Wardle was speaking.

'We'd better go up to see *Captain S/M,*' he said; 'he doesn't like being kept waiting.' As they made their way up to the Captain's cabin under the bridge no words passed; it was clear that the Commander and the Captain were not on the closest possible terms of friendship.

At the door the Commander stood back and waved him on. Tommy gave a perfunctory knock and walked in.

Captain Sanderson was sitting at his roll-top desk with his back to the door. If he heard the knock he gave no sign, nor did he turn as Tommy entered and shut the door behind him.

'*Gauntlet* secured alongside, sir,' said Tommy in a clear voice. Sanderson turned on his revolving chair and looked at him in silence for a while.

Presently he spoke in a hard crisp voice. 'Any defects?' he asked.

'Nothing of importance, sir,' said Tommy.

'Crew healthy?'

'All very fit, sir.'

'Good.' A silence. Then: 'We've lost the *Gordian*.'

'So I hear.'

'You will have to take her place; I can give you two days in harbour.'

'That's plenty, sir.'

'Five weeks patrol, including going there and coming back. Can do?'

'Can do.'

'All right. Come to the staff office at nine o'clock tomorrow morning.'

'Aye, aye, sir.' Tommy turned to go, when Sanderson spoke again.

'You knew Carter?'

'He was my best friend, sir.'

'Good chap. Perhaps you'd write to his people. Got his address?'

'Oh yes. I married his sister.'

'Did you? Not much of a reception to greet you with, that. Still. There it is. Tomorrow morning then.'

Once more Tommy turned to go.

'You did well in the Mediterranean,' said *Captain S/M*, 'it isn't quite so easy out here.'

That was all. Tommy walked out feeling as if he had been caught in the act of blowing his own trumpet and had been rightly reproved. He wasn't aware that he'd given any evidence of a swelled head, why he hadn't even put his medal ribbons up. Deep in thought he descended to the upper deck and found Shiner waiting for him.

'You look exactly like a chap who has been talking to *Captain S/M*,' he said quietly.

Tommy grinned weakly. 'Is he always like that?' he asked.

'Always,' said Shiner. 'If the entire Japanese fleet surrendered to him personally he'd still take a pessimistic view of the situation. He spends the whole of his time touching wood and crossing his fingers as he does so. Actually he's a good chap to serve under. No fancy nonsense; and if you get in a hole he'll go bail for you every time. But I do wish that sometimes he'd smile. Still, you can't have everything. Still got the same First-Lieutenant?'

'Yes,' said Tommy.

'Lucky devil,' said Shiner, 'I've a new bloke, very intellectual. Do you know what a Brains Trust is?'

'Something to do with the radio, isn't it?'

'Blessed if I know. But he's always talking about it *and* he reads those A.B.C.A. pamphlets – nothing but red propaganda. Still, he's fairly reliable, but I do miss my poker parties. Heigho. Bad show about George. Audrey won't like it a bit, will she?'

'No,' said Tommy, 'not a bit. How's your wife?'

'Annette? Grousing a bit. Wants me to chuck submarines. Queer people, women. She's expecting in a month from now. Makes 'em fanciful, I suppose.'

'I suppose so. Why aren't you on patrol?'

'Waiting for a new part. It's being flown out from England. The first lot fell in the pond. The second one didn't fit and the third has been diverted to Bombay. In the meantime I wait patiently in harbour. Did you bring any gin with you?'

'I could only get a case. It's awfully short in Alex.'

'Did you say *only* a case?' said Shiner. 'We've been on one bottle of beer per head per diem for the last month. A case! Boy, oh boy. What about a little party, eh?'

'Come down to the boat at six o'clock,' said Tommy, 'we're off on patrol in forty-eight hours. I must go and break the glad news to Number One. I fancy he won't be very pleased.'

'O.K.,' said Shiner, 'but a case! What is it, Plymouth? Not that it matters. I'd drink methylated spirit if there was any.' He went away and Tommy went back to his submarine, where the news that *Gauntlet* was next on patrol had already reached the crew and Bill Brown's comments verged on the mutinous.

'Three weeks at sea and two days in harbour. It's a bit thick, sir.'

'I suppose it is,' said Tommy, 'but don't go beefing about it.

We're a new chicken in this run and can expect to be pecked a bit.'

Bill grinned. 'Sorry, sir.'

'That's all right,' said Tommy, 'I'd be a good deal more fed up about it myself if it wasn't for the news of the *Gordian* – my brother-in-law was her skipper.'

'I didn't know,' said Bill.

'So you see,' said Tommy, 'I feel like having a crack at the bastards who did him in, and the sooner the quicker.'

'I'll have a word with the cox'n on those lines,' said Bill, 'he's been expressing his opinion of this flotilla a trifle more broadly than I have.'

'Yes, do,' said Tommy and changed the subject.

'By the way,' he said. 'I've a confession to make. I let it be known that we have a case of gin. I feel that we may have a few visitors at six o'clock precisely.'

Bill grinned. 'So do I,' he said, 'it's all over the ship already. I'd better borrow some glasses. The poor devils haven't tasted gin for three weeks.'

'Put on your drinking boots,' said Tommy, 'we're in for a wet, wild evening, while the stuff lasts.'

'I've a request from the P.O. Tel., sir, to see you privately,' added Bill.

'What's Toogood's trouble?' asked Tommy.

Bill hesitated. 'He wouldn't say anything to me, sir, but it looks as if he's cracking up.'

'What makes you think that?'

'I don't know; just a feeling.'

'Well,' said Tommy, 'send him along to my cabin, it's number twenty-three I'm told. I'll see him right away.'

He went down in search of, and found, his cabin, where an officer's steward was making up his bunk and unpacking his traps. Tommy worked with him until there was a knock on the door and then he dismissed the man and called for Petty Officer Toogood to come in.

'What's the trouble, Toogood?'

'I've got the wind up, sir.'

'Is that all; who hasn't?'

'I've got a feeling, sir, that we're for it next time. I don't think I can go, sir.'

Tommy looked at the man curiously. He knew Toogood as an exceedingly efficient telegraphist. He knew he was married and mildly red in his politics, but beyond that he knew nothing about him.

'What are you trying to do, Toogood,' he asked, 'put the wind up me as well?'

'I got a premonition, sir,' said Toogood.

'I always have one before going to sea. How are you sleeping?'

'Pretty fair, sir, only I keep dreaming of water comin' in through a hole in the hull and I'm trying to hold it out. It squirts past and floods the switchboard and all the lights go out and I wake up yelling blue murder.'

'Jolly little dream,' said Tommy, 'I shall probably dream it myself tonight, instead of my particular one, which is that I'm stuck at periscope-depth just under the bows of a destroyer and I can't get her down and I can't see through the periscope. On the whole I prefer yours. Any other troubles? How are things at home?'

'All right,' said Toogood.

'Nothing else on your mind?'

'No, sir.'

'Well,' said Tommy, 'you're absolutely right. You've got the wind up. So have I, so has everybody.'

' 'Ave they, sir?'

'Sure,' said Tommy, 'pretty nearly. There are a few thick-headed chaps who are too bloody stupid to know when they're afraid, but that's about all. There's no harm in being afraid unless you let it make you run away. If it does that you've had it. "The coward dies a thousand deaths" – you know the rest. Get the idea? What makes you think that not going to sea with us is any good? You'll be bloody miserable if you report sick and see us trundling out without you, and then you'll get the wind up worse and worse at everything that happens to you, until you eventually fall out of bed and break your flaming neck. What a life! Tell you what. Every time you feel it coming on tell yourself – "what the hell, brother; we've all got to die sometime". It has a calming effect; that's what I find.'

A light came into Toogood's eyes.

'You do, sir?'

'Why not? It's natural enough to be afraid of dying. Did you volunteer for this lot?'

'Yes, sir.'

'Why?'

'I don't really know.'

'You don't really know very much, but I will say you're a good telegraphist. What do you want me to do; send you to a "trick cyclist" who will put you on a couch and get you to talk about yourself and then diagnose nerve strain? I will if you really want me to. Hold out your hands; let's see if your fingers have got the wind up.'

Toogood stretched out his arms and fingers. They showed no tendency to shake.

'Better than mine,' said Tommy. 'What's it to be, run away, or face it?'

'Face it, sir. I feel better for talking to you. I thought I was the only chap like – like this.'

'I'll lay you half a dollar you don't dream that one again,' said Tommy. 'You've chosen the right way. This is the hell of a war but it's damn' nearly over. I'll do my best to keep us all alive; I'm a married man, you know.'

'I didn't know, sir.'

'Makes me cautious.'

'I hadn't noticed that, sir,' Toogood grinned.

'No?'

'Can I go now, sir?'

'Just a minute. Have you a religion?'

'Not much, sir. I don't 'old with it.'

'I thought not. Pity. Yes, carry on.'

Toogood went out and Tommy sat down to write to his wife and George Carter's sister. He started three different letters and then abandoned the thing. For the first time in his married life he couldn't find the heart to write to Audrey. All very well pulling that big-brother stuff over Toogood. Some men loved being wet-nursed, but Audrey was going to take the loss of her brother very hard indeed. She had been a devoted sister. His loss in a submarine would double her anxiety for her husband. For a moment or two Tommy played with the idea of leaving submarines as some sort of recompense for his wife's loss, but, as he did so, he knew that Audrey wouldn't permit it. Anyway, he was in no mood for letter writing. He went out and down to his command to begin the gin-session, for it was past six o'clock, and already a thin stream of casually-walking officers was making its way across the gang-planks, like the forerunners of some colony of ants.

Shiner was already on board. He had taken up a strategic position on the wardroom settee next to the bottle and had his nose half-way inside a beaker of gin.

'I couldn't wait, Tommy,' he said, 'besides you're late.'

'Manners!' said Tommy.

'Can I come in?' said Commander Wardle rubbing his hands with anticipatory delight.

'Hullo, Tommy old boy,' said another voice, while others were greeting Bill Brown and Morgan Jones.

'What a lot of friends we have this evening,' said Tommy, 'where's Mr Miles?'

'In the control-room; addressing an overflow meeting of the plumbers' union,' said Bill. 'He's got a bottle with him.'

'So I imagined,' said Tommy.

Some time later the wardroom flunkey and the First-Lieutenant stood surveying the smoking ashtrays and empty glasses.

'Nothin' but a swarm of bloody locusts,' said the First-Lieutenant.

'I kept back a bottle, sir,' said Davies.

'Good lad,' said Bill, 'we'll have it when we get back from patrol. It'll be something to look forward to when we get back.'

CHAPTER THREE

PREPARING a submarine for a long war patrol is a considerable business, especially when there are only forty-eight hours in which to do it.

While Tommy went to the staff office to be briefed, the rest of the officers and ship's company never let up. Bill Brown, his head pulsating with the unaccustomed superfluity of gin, was hard put to it to see his way to be ready in time. His main trouble was that the *Gauntlet*'s electric batteries required 'topping up' with distilled water. This meant that the 'floors' of the two compartments had to be lifted while the electrical staff wielded a fresh-water hose directing a few pints of specially tested water into each of the three hundred and thirty-three cells, comprising the three storage batteries. After topping up, the cells must be wiped over, and the connections greased; then they must be charged until the new distilled water was thoroughly mixed with the electrolyte. All this business, with the floorboards lifted, interfered completely with traffic in the submarine, but it must be done, for the submarine's battery was its life-blood when submerged. Meanwhile there were twelve torpedoes to be got ready in the fore compartment which could only be approached by way of one of the compartments in which the 'road was up'. Likewise the Chief wished to strip and renew certain parts of his engine but must keep one engine available for charging the batteries as soon as the topping up ceremony was completed.

Likewise one of the periscopes in the control-room was in need of desiccation; this entailed the attachment of a special air-drying plant in a compartment where the floor was missing.

Likewise some extra ammunition was needed, and as for provisions, Guts Hinton had them stacked on deck in the hot sizzling rain, crates and crates of tinned food and no chance of stowing it until the battery floors were replaced.

Morgan Jones, deprived of the use of the wardroom table, now tied up out of the way of the battery workers, was fretting and fuming at being unable to get his charts in order for the trip. Thus, for the first part of that day the only people able to get on with the maintenance work in the submarine were the wireless operators and the gunlayers who, perspiring in oilskins, were stripping and cleaning their weapons on deck in the pouring rain. The prospect of six weeks' tropical routine in a submarine was not an encouraging one, without this mad scamper to get ready and so, though everybody was working hard, tempers were a little frayed. Guts Hinton, in particular, was giving vent to some pretty caustic stuff.

'Good job we arrived when we did,' he was saying, for all to hear, 'otherwise this war would 'ave stopped dead. Three boats in harbour and they have to pick on us. What's that in that sack – you there, Davis?'

Bert Davis, laden with wardroom stores, stopped and stood balancing precariously on the swaying gang-plank.

'What do you think,' he asked – 'it's just a sack of coal in case of anybody gettin' cold feet.'

'That's quite enough from you,' said the coxswain, delighted with a bit of cockney repartee, 'what are you feeding 'em on this time, brick-bats?'

'I'm not relying on you for any comforts,' said Bert. A passing destroyer's wake nearly upset him into the water. ''Ere,' he said plaintively, 'give us a hand, 'swain, we're fighting on the same side in this war, aren't we?'

'If I was the skipper,' said Guts, 'I'd have something to say about bein' sent out as soon as look at us. Lazy lot of baskets – loafin' in 'arbour. They ought to 'ave been in the Med in our flotilla – they'd have learnt somethin' about war. Ought to be ashamed of 'emselves – now don't be all night toppin' up that blasted battery, 'Arry!'

Petty Officer Felton appeared at the bottom of the torpedo hatch. He was wearing bathing trunks and was streaming with sweat. 'Wot's up, 'swain?' he asked.

'Nothin's up,' said the coxswain, 'I said, "don't be all night." I want to get my stores in.'

'The longer you stand there wastin' my time,' said 'Arry Felton, 'the wetter you'll get. Come down and give us a 'and.'

'I've somethin' better to do than piddle into a lot of blasted cells,' said the coxswain.

'Gauntlet! Gauntlet!' A supply Petty Officer was hailing the submarine from the *Carpentaria* – 'send along to the victualling store for fresh provisions.'

'I can't send now, 'aven't got any 'ands and if I 'ad any 'ands I couldn't get the stuff on board. Can't you see? Or are you ruddy-well barmy? After dinner!' bawled the coxswain.

'*Gauntlet* ahoy!'

'Now what is it?'

It was Tommy. 'Tell the Navigator to come to my cabin with the charts!'

'Aye, aye, sir.' The coxswain saluted. 'And take that grin off your face, young Davis,' he added out of the corner of his mouth, 'or you won't see a half a gill for a fortnight. Better go and 'elp the navigator with 'is charts,' he added, 'he's not very good on the planks, especially after last night.'

'Wot do you mean,' said Bert Davis, in arms on behalf of his officers – 'they was all as sober as judges – 'ad to be; them blasted depot-ship people came and swiped the lot.'

'I don't know why I joined this perishin' outfit,' said the coxswain, apropos of nothing.

'You shouldn't 'ave if you can't take a joke,' said Davis, moving off. 'Don't go pinching my stores – I've given my signature for that lot.'

'How are you getting on?' asked Bill Brown, appearing from nowhere.

'Gettin' on splendid, sir,' said the coxswain, 'I don't think. What's all the perishin' 'urry about; anyone would think we'd got plague on board us.'

'That's enough beefing from you,' said Bill. 'You'd better go and make your peace with that supply Chief Petty Officer, he says you were rude to him.'

'I never said a thing,' said the coxswain piously. 'Cor! what a flotilla. Can't talk politely to a feller without 'im runnin' to 'is mother. They ought to 'ave been in the Med.'

So it went on. While they worked and sweated and swore they could just see the end in view and they knew from long experience that the submarine would be ready in time. Bill Brown with a long list of items to be seen to, was satisfied with the progress, but kept urging greater speed, and the day passed only too quickly.

Up in the staff office Tommy was being well and truly briefed.

Lieutenant Commander Twiggs, R.N.V.R., was a perfect

example of that type of intellectual which seems to gravitate naturally to intelligence work. He gave the impression of being closely in the confidence of Messrs Winston Churchill and Roosevelt, and referred to members of the Higher Command by their christian names. That he was a student of global warfare there was no doubt at all. He prefaced his briefing of Tommy's patrol by a round-the-world survey of the war situation, to put Tommy, as it were, in the picture.

Tommy, who rather naturally had himself taken a considerable interest in the war, found himself listening to a schoolmasterly dissertation on pincer movements, strategic withdrawals and psychological warfare; that is, for the first few minutes, but presently his attention strayed from his well-intentioned tutor and he began to think of his own personal problems. What was he to say to Audrey about her brother? Why was it so difficult to think at all about it? Why couldn't he sit down and say what was in his mind? George Carter, in spite of, or because of being his brother-in-law, had been one of his best friends; the bond, therefore, between Tommy and Audrey could only be strengthened by their common loss. It ought to be easy enough to write but it wasn't going to be. He'd half a mind to write omitting all reference to George before sailing on patrol. When he returned the wound would no longer be so painful, he could pretend he hadn't heard before about the *Gordian*; perhaps if he postponed writing he would never have to do it at all; perhaps it was his turn to go next – if that happened how could Audrey face this double loss? He shivered.

'There is little doubt that by the spring of nineteen forty-four we shall be in a position to mount an offensive on the largest scale,' Twiggs was saying. 'Between ourselves,' he winked through his pebble-thick glasses, 'between ourselves something considerable is in the wind. I can't say more, you understand?'

'But what has all this to do with *Gauntlet*'s operation?' asked Tommy.

'I'm coming to that,' said Twiggs.

'Well, make it snappy,' said Tommy, 'I've some letters to write.' His mind was suddenly made up. He would write and tell Audrey how he felt about it. It was the only possible thing to do. Twiggs looked for a moment as if he was going to cry.

'I thought,' he said, 'you'd like to be given the broadest

possible view of the world situation. So many commanding officers complain that they have not been put in the picture.'

'Oh, that's all right, old boy,' said Tommy, 'but the fact is I'm a bit rushed for time. When I come back from this patrol you can give me the whole works, but just now you tell me what I've got to do.'

It turned out to be a simple enough task – an offensive patrol in the vicinity of Port Blair, the principal port of the Andaman Islands; but even this straightforward duty had to be covered up by such expressions as 'probing attacks', 'offensive spirit', 'keeping the enemy on his toes', etc. Boiled down, it required *Gauntlet* to observe and report all hostile movements and to attack suitable targets whenever they presented themselves, but Twiggs wasn't letting it go at that.

'The enemy's endurance,' he said impressively, emphasising his words with rhythmic strokes of an H.B. pencil, 'is known to be taxed to the limit; it may well be that some successes by *Gauntlet* will cause the first crack which will bring the whole fabric of Japanese might crumbling to the ground. I cannot say more.' But he could have, and would have, if Captain Sanderson had not arrived at the moment.

He walked in silently, grunted a good morning and stood staring at the chart. Presently he spoke.

'Any questions?' he asked.

'What is the torpedo situation out here?' asked Tommy. 'Can I expend as much as I like?'

Captain S/M nodded. 'When in doubt attack,' he said. 'The Japs have had it too much their own way; supplies are coming through far more plentifully than they did; and don't forget you've got a gun.'

'What about aircraft?' asked Tommy.

'Considerable strength,' said the Captain, 'though not of the first quality; after the Mediterranean you may find them ineffectual. Has Twiggs given you the broad strategy of the picture?'

'Very much so,' said Tommy.

Captain Sanderson shot a rapid glance at him. 'We like our captains to be given the fullest possible information,' he said. 'I'll send your orders over later today.' He went to the door. 'Good hunting,' he said and went out.

'Where was I?' said Twiggs.

'Never mind,' said Tommy, 'I really must go.'

He left his mentor blinking sadly through his glasses, and went straight to his cabin.

'Dear Audrey' (he wrote)

'Isn't it bloody about poor George. I am thoroughly shaken up. He was so much alive and reminded me so much of you. I wish you were here to tell me how you feel, but perhaps when I return from our next patrol you will have wangled a passage. In the meantime you may count on me to take extra care of my precious skin. This is an odd flotilla, full of odd types, but they seem nice enough. Shiner is here, as mad as ever, and sends his love. I am off again tomorrow on what promises to be the dullest and safest thing I've done so far. Six weeks in a Turkish bath! When you do come try and bring some gin with you – this is almost a dry country, the dirty dogs swiped all mine last night. Our skipper seems a pompous old bit of housework, but means well.

'No time for more. They thought the world of George here and are very cut up, but the war must go on – (to coin a phrase).

'You'd laugh at our staff-officer, straight out of a book.

'Oh, Audrey, I love you.

'Your own Tommy.'

He felt better after that.

CHAPTER FOUR

A PARALLEL can be drawn between the lot of the common angler and that of the simple submariner. In the former case an early riser may observe him setting out heavily laden with his paraphernalia, usually on a wet and windy day. He probably walks to the corner, boards a tram and disappears from anybody's ken. He returns unheralded, more often with the traditional 'wet arse and no fish' than not, but occasionally he has something to show for his labours and once in a blue moon he may be awarded a prize for the biggest fish of the week.

So it is with the submariner. For every prize awarded for a 'big fish' there are weeks of wet, dangerous and unrewarding work, during which the morale of the submarine's crew must be kept well boosted, otherwise, when the opportunity at long last presents itself, they will be too slow to grasp it, and the big fish will get away.

Perhaps, therefore, it was a good thing that the *Gauntlet*'s crew had no time to listen to the discouraging stories brought back from patrol by the other submarines. Hunting was not good in the Indian Ocean at that time. Targets were few and small, distances were great and at the time of the S.W. monsoon the weather was perpetually wet and windy. The conditions in a submarine in this constant atmosphere of hot humidity were enervating and distinctly depressing. It was almost as much as the average man could do to keep himself healthy, and, then, when he returned to his depot-ship and found little but much-delayed letters from home, full of the usual wartime grouses, it became a major problem to get him to snap out of his lethargy.

Certainly there was no time for lethargy in *Gauntlet*, for things were going wrong all over the place. To begin at the fore-end of the vessel, Joe Parker, the worthy Torpedo Gunner's Mate, was in trouble. One of his torpedoes had developed an air leak which would not be cured. The trouble was that Joe had wasted four hours trying to cure it, at the end of which it was necessary to rig the embarkation rails and to hoist the beastly thing out in exchange for another from the depot-ship. This operation took the best part of another hour, at the end of which the new torpedo was found to have a similar defect, and had to be exchanged for yet another one. Tempers were frayed to the limit by this misfortune and time began to run out. Bill Brown, silent but always about, looked at his wristwatch and decided that it was going to be a close thing to be ready by four o'clock that afternoon, but he kept his counsel and wandered aft to see how the Chief was faring. The engine-room looked even less ready. Parts of the port engine were lying all over the place, for Mr Miles, in the course of a routine examination, had found a cracked piston which he was replacing by means of chain purchases, awning tackles and much bad language, which was drowned by the roar of the other engine as it ceaselessly drove the dynamos which were charging *Gauntlet*'s electric batteries. Little Izzy Sammons was in a rare paddy to judge by the way his lips were working, while Mr Miles, unable to smoke his beloved pipe, because the batteries were on charge, was sucking at the thing in a dispirited manner.

On the little chart table, between the hydroplane wheels in the control-room, Morgan Jones was flogging out the sailing orders which had just come in, while at his elbow Bert Toogood was scribbling industriously, things like wave-lengths, recognition signals, and the like. Under the Navigator's legs an Able Seaman was trying to take the density of the battery through a small hand aperture; and a little to the left two members of the engine-room department were grinding in a leaky air valve. In the middle of everything the desiccator was breathing heavily through the after periscope. And all the time raindrops poured down the open conning-tower hatch with a depressing constancy.

In the Petty Officers' Mess Guts Hinton was leisurely filling in the various forms, which accounted for the expenditure of rum and comforts. He worked rather like a schoolboy doing home-work, with his tongue curling out of his mouth and his pen inscribing some utterly fictional figures in the best standard-seven copperplate.

On deck the oilskinned figures of the gun-layers were to be observed wiping off and regreasing their breechwork for the umpteenth time. Things were progressing, reflected Bill Brown, but it was going to be touch and go. Then, to make matters worse, the inside submarine of the 'trot' expressed a keen desire to go out on trials and would not be denied. To let her out required the use of both propellers – and meant the breaking of the charge as well as the attendance on deck of a number of men to handle the berthing wires. Bill excused the main working parties and made do with those men whom he thought could be spared, but who, of course, thought otherwise. Then the skipper of the inside submarine was delayed by a last minute call to speak to the *Captain S/M*, and they were all kept kicking their heels in the pouring rain. At last, when the inside submarine did go, there was an unseemly scramble to get back alongside as soon as she had slipped out astern, the result of which was that the wind and tide caught the submarines' bows and forced them away from the depot-ship. Then the tails came in and the inside one hit the *Carpentaria* such a nudge that it brought the Commanding Officer on deck, attended by the Second-in-Command and an obsequious Staff Officer. This nudge was retransmitted to *Gauntlet* who was lying third alongside. Bill Brown felt it and reckoned that the next boat's after hydroplane had slid under his own and had struck the *Gauntlet*'s rudder a considerable blow. Consequently he went below and, putting the steering gear into 'hand' he worked it through the limits of its travel, to see if anything was damaged. It worked freely for two-thirds of the way and then got stiff; it was not very stiff, and he wondered whether it was worth bothering about. Then he decided it was and called in the technical staff. They stripped the gear and gave it a good oiling, and it worked more freely; but there was still that tight spot which could not be remedied inside the submarine. To rectify this would necessitate a visit to the floating dock, and that was a matter for the Captain to decide.

Tommy heard the disquieting news with a certain amount of scepticism. So often had he known the occurrence of a defect just before the vessel was due to sail. It wasn't that his subordinates manufactured them, but it seemed that they were rather anxious to exploit their possibilities. A visit to the floating dock meant two more days in harbour. They weren't malingerers, but – well, you know how it is?

So Tommy went on board and worked the steering-gear himself by hand. Then he switched it into electric drive and worked it by power, observing the amount of current which the motor took.

It wasn't quite right; at the tight spot the needle flickered up to twice the normal load for only a second. Tommy worked it a dozen times, resolved that if the fuse blew he would have to delay his sailing. Twelve times the gear worked successfully and he decided that it would do. If he had worked it a little more this story would not have been written.

Tommy returned to the *Carpentaria* to smoke and yarn in the mess, for it is the unwritten law that the Captain does not board his command until the actual time of sailing. However much he may prefer to do otherwise he must wait nonchalantly until the right moment has come.

Meanwhile Bill Brown stood at the door of the torpedo-room waiting to check the important 'settings' on each torpedo as it was launched in. He could have delegated this work but never did; he reckoned that he slept better at night if he had personally checked all the important things aboard.

At one minute to four the Captain stepped aboard and the gang-plank splashed into the water behind him. Bill Brown saluted and reported ready for sea; Mr Miles saluted and reported both engines ready, and Morgan Jones reported that all sailing orders, codes and signals were on board. The Captain nodded his acknowledgement and climbed on to the bridge.

He gave two orders.

'Let go!' and 'Half speed astern together.' Slowly the *Gauntlet* gathered stern-way and slipped away from the *Carpentaria.* Nobody watched her go – there was nothing to watch and the rain was falling ceaselessly. A small wet submarine lay stopped astern of the depot-ship awhile, and then suddenly a burst of smoke and a flurry of propeller-wash showed at her tail. She began to move ahead, slowly at first and then, as she gathered way, she listed under the turning influence of her rudder and went rapidly out of harbour into the mist and rain.

The Staff Officer took a piece of chalk and wrote on his board. 'Sailed sixteen hundred. 12/8/43;' then he dismissed *Gauntlet* from his mind, and began to write an appreciation of the situation in the Far East, a much more interesting study than this humdrum task of sending submariners out on patrol.

CHAPTER FIVE

As soon as the outer gate-vessel had been passed the *Gauntlet* fell in astern of her escort destroyer, whose task was to guard her against the well-intended vigilance of her friends. The rule was that all submarines are to be considered hostile unless they prove themselves otherwise; consequently a friendly escort was the only protection against patrolling ships and aircraft who were notoriously trigger-happy.

At the end of four hours' steady steaming the escort hoisted a signal. 'Proceed in execution of previous orders,' waited a pause, hauled the signal down, and set off in the reverse direction at a hand-gallop. *Gauntlet* went on her ten-knot way, a lone submarine. From now on she must depend upon herself entirely. Seven hundred miles ahead was her objective; now all vessels encountered must be avoided and the Captain would not know a restful moment until he was once more under the care of his escort; and much was going to happen before that.

Although it was now dark Tommy decided to follow his invariable practice of getting his ship underwater as soon as possible after leaving harbour. Since the only safety for the submarine lay in its ability to disappear at will into its element, the first thing to do was to make sure that all was well with her diving powers.

Since she had last dived the *Gauntlet* had embarked some tons of provisions, explosives and drinking water. She had completed with oil-fuel, and 'topped up' her batteries, and all this meant that the weight of the vessel was different from that with which she dived before arrival at her base.

It was Bill Brown's job in harbour to work out the differences of weight, and to compensate for them by altering the amount of internal ballast water carried. This was quite a simple mathematical problem, provided the Chief Stoker had measured the amount of water in the ballast tanks accurately, and provided that the weight of gear brought on board could be computed. Bill usually got the answer right, but the first dive after leaving harbour was always likely to be an interesting one. For that reason Tommy did not press the button of the diving hooter. Instead he stopped his engines, sent everybody down below and then descending through the conning-tower hatch-way, closed the hatch behind him and gave the order to dive.

It was just as well that he did so, for, as soon as *Gauntlet* began to run under, it was clear that she was very heavy. Down went her bows; the bubbles in the spirit-levels shot aft, the pointers of the diving gauges moved round in no uncertain manner, and before Tommy could order: 'Shut main vents,' the submarine was heading for a hundred feet at ever increasing speed.

Tommy waited for a moment to see if the 'planes would hold her up and then, seeing that she was out of control, gave the order to blow three of the main ballast tanks.

Immediately the valves were opened, and air screamed into the main ballast tanks. The needles of the diving gauges faltered in their rotary motion and then halted.

'Stop blowing,' ordered Tommy. He caught Bill's eye. 'Error,' he said, 'appears to have crept in.'

'I can't understand it,' said Bill.

'Did you take a density of the water?' asked Tommy.

Bill hung his head. 'No,' he said.

'Well, take one now,' said his Captain. 'Pumps on "A", "Z" and "Number six auxiliary".'

While he supervised this routine business of getting the submarine into correct trim, bringing her back to sixty feet and adjusting matters so that she would hold her depth with only one propeller going slow ahead, Tommy had time to think that it was a good thing to have got under water when he had. An involuntary plunge in the face of the enemy wouldn't have been half so funny; this little bit of nonsense was just what was required to steady up his crew and bring them out of the realms of discontent and nostalgia. He looked round the control-room with real satisfaction at seeing the same familiar faces, or rather backsides, (for most of the men had to face their apparatus which was always fixed on a bulkhead on the ship's hull). 'If I was an artist,' he reflected, 'I would draw those views as being far more expressive than any face. Guts Hinton, for example; a bald head, three folds of fat on bull-like neck, a sweat-soaked shirt, looking like the top half of a cottage loaf, and then an enormous blue bottom mounted on a diminutive music stool, the whole statue indicative of strength of purpose, pugnacity and imperturbability.'

'Next to him Badger, the second coxswain, lounging gracefully on his little seat – looking more like a tired and dirty Russian dancer than an Acting-Petty Officer – every motion a rhythmic one. Between those two stalwarts the navigator crouches over his chart staring at it as if he expects it to reveal some hidden secret and sitting in front of the gyro-compass-repeater the helmsman, Williams, with a perpetual sniff, turns his steering wheel with an economy of movement that only long experience will allow.'

They were all part of a living frieze which moved and acted as ordered by Tommy, or Bill who would take over from the skipper when Tommy said: 'All right, Number One.' From now on, until they once more returned to harbour, every action of each man might decide whether they were going to continue to live or whether they would join their colleagues of the *Gordian* and alas, many other ships. Such a common bond is rare enough; no wonder it was unnecessary to maintain the sort of discipline which calls for uniformity of dress, haircuts and saluting.

They looked a pretty crowd of pirates already – what would they look like in six weeks time?

Number One, who had paid a visit to the privy for the purpose of drawing off sea water from the flood valve, returned with a hydrometer pot in which was floating the gadget for measuring the density of the sea.

'It's damn nearly fresh,' he said, giving the reading.

'Not surprising,' said his Captain, 'considering it's been raining for six weeks. You'll have to watch it from now on, we're not in the Mediterranean now.'

Bill accepted the rebuke, which was well merited, and presently was allowed to take over the adjustment of the trim and Tommy, as was his usual custom, went wandering round the submarine for the purpose of showing himself to the men whose diving stations kept them in complete ignorance of what was going on. These were the men on whom a great deal would depend in emergency. They were not sitting under the eyes of these officers. Orders would reach them through the 'intercom,' but no explanation with them. The wrong valve opened at the crucial moment could spoil a torpedo attack, or betray the existence of *Gauntlet* by bubble, or make an oil-slick. It was a good thing to let them see the Captain pottering round his ship; it stopped them from feeling neglected. Getting a crew to pull as one required a little more than firm direction, it also required humanity.

Aft in the engine-room, that ghostly compartment which seemed to reek of regrets for the cessation of the hideous roar of Diesels, the engine-room staff were gazing gloomily at a few pressure gauges, whilst Mr Miles and Izzy Sammons were doing something with feeler-gauges in a preoccupied manner. Tommy passed them by and entered the motor-room. He never ceased to marvel at the ability of his men to stand the temperature in this compartment. It must have been well over a hundred. The two operators sitting back to back on canvas camp stools facing the giant chopper switches and ammeters which formed the motor switch-boards, were clad in short trunks, sweat was running down their bare bodies in continuous streams. Their hair lay lank on their foreheads, their eyes swimming in sweat watched the motor telegraphs.

'Warm enough?' asked Tommy.

They grinned and one of them spoke.

'Puts me in mind of that time off Pantellaria when we got the U-boat,' he said, 'though I reckon it was hotter nor this.'

The other one added his contribution, for which Tommy was waiting. 'It isn't the 'eat so much, sir, it's the 'umidity.'

'Too right,' said Tommy, as he passed on, 'anyway you're not wearing your clothes out.'

They grinned and nodded to each other, a silent confirmation that the skipper was just the same as usual. A word and a joke for everyone. It wasn't so bad, they felt, to have to do this sort of thing with that sort of man.

Beyond the motor-room was a cramped compartment from which came the sounds of a ballast pump mixed with the whine of the turning propeller shafts. Two stokers squatted thoughtfully there, surrounded entirely by pipes and valves, their feet in a pool of oil and water.

'What's this?' demanded Tommy.

'Stern gland,' said one, 'I've nipped it up now.'

'D'you like paddling?' asked Tommy.

The men grinned sheepishly. 'We was just going to mop

it up, sir,' one said and then turned to his mate. 'Go and ask the Chief E.R.A. for a bit o' waste and get a bucket from behind the port engine.'

Tommy moved away, wondering how long they'd have stopped where they were before mustering up the energy to clean up the mess.

Back in the engine room he spoke to Mr Miles. 'Bit of a snipe-marsh in the after compartment, Chief,' and passed on, secure in the knowledge that he hadn't wasted his visit.

Just abaft the control-room proper, was housed the wireless officer and the Asdic cabinet, hot, airless little compartments where the 'ears' of the submarine were controlled.

Bert Toogood was polishing a bit of brass with feverish energy and looked a bit shamed-faced as his Captain entered. Tommy decided to ignore any recollection of the last time he and Toogood had been together.

'Shove up,' he said, and seating himself alongside the Petty Officer Telegraphist, he catechised him on such matters as wave-lengths, frequencies and routine listening periods, all of which information was contained in the sailing orders. Toogood seemed to have it all at his finger-tips and Tommy passed on with a curt nod. The man was all right.

Next was the Asdic cabinet where its sole occupant was operating a large wheel which controlled the direction of the Asdic beam – a supersonic ray which would send back an echo if it struck any object in the water.

'Nothing at all, sir,' said the operator as he turned his wheel another ten degrees. 'I've swept right round. There's nothing there.'

'Any false echoes?' asked Tommy.

'Nothin' at all,' said the operator. 'Nothin' at all.'

Tommy went away.

Forward now to the torpedo room with its six spare 'fish' in their racks, shining with grease like great sardines. The tube's crew were squatting silently in a quiet compartment in which the whine of the fore-hydroplane and an occasional sound of the water flowing over the hull were the only noises.

Joe Parker, the Torpedo Gunner's Mate, tired, after forty-eight hours' continuous work on the torpedoes, got stiffly to his feet and gave a slightly over-punctilious report. 'Everything correct, sir.'

Tommy said: 'Thank you, Parker,' and went away. The

man was feeling bloody-minded, and needed a good night's rest more than anything.

At the wardroom 'galley' the 'flunkey' quickly switched off the oven in which was reposing a cottage pie. Tommy tactfully ignored this breach of his orders that there was to be no cooking whilst diving, and went back to the control-room.

By now the *Gauntlet* was in perfect trim, diving at her set depth, idling along at less than one knot. Bill Brown looked a little ostentatiously at his wrist-watch as his Captain entered. It was late and they had all had a long day, his gesture implied. Tommy went to a round box by the conning-tower ladder from which protruded a red button. He placed his finger on it and held it there whilst the raucous note of klaxons sounded throughout the submarine.

This was the signal for emergency change of depth – to be obeyed instantly and with maximum effort. No sooner had the sound of the diving-hooter ceased than the effect of this emergency order made itself felt. The *Gauntlet*'s bows dipped sharply under the influence of Guts and Badger, the main motor indicated lights glowed at 'full-speed' and the whole ship trembled under the mighty thrust of her propellors. Tommy flicked a stop watch and watched the second hand running round. 'One hundred and thirty,' he ordered.

The depth gauge needles were moving now almost as fast as the stop-watch hand. Gut's voice intoned the depth changes at every ten feet.

'Ninety,' he said, ' 'undred, 'undred and ten,' – 'Level off!' ordered Tommy. 'Level off, sir, 'undred and twenty.' The needles slowed down and quivered at a hundred and thirty.

Tommy ordered slow speed again and held her at that depth whilst Mr Miles and Bill went round looking for leaks. When they were satisfied that there were none the *Gauntlet* was brought slowly to sixty feet.

'Getting on for supper-time,' observed Number One, apropos of nothing. Tommy blandly ignored him, pressed the hooter again and once more gained the depths at maximum speed. Then, and only then, after returning to sixty feet, did he decide to call it a day.

The Asdic operator, having once more repeated 'nothin' at all,' the submarine was brought to periscope depth. Then with the order of 'Surface!' Tommy watched the actions of his highly trained crew with a good deal of satisfaction. It was all very slick. Bill Brown gave some orders – air screamed into the ballast tanks – Guts wound his hydro-plane wheel to hard-a-rise – the depth gauge pointers wound rapidly to the surface – Tommy climbed the conning-tower ladder and threw open the hatch as the words 'five feet!' sounded in his ear. Immediately as he scrambled on to the dark and dripping bridge he felt the first kick of the main engines as they coughed to life and started once more to suck air through the conning-tower. Closely following upon Tommy's heels came the signalman with night glasses, a 'Very' pistol and other equipment for night cruising. Tommy climbed high up on the periscope standards and searched all round him in the blackness of the tropical night. It was still raining and he could see nothing, save the phosphorescence of the water as it washed over the *Gauntlet*'s saddle-tanks, and the occasional breaking crest of a wave. The air was saturated with moisture, and yet the small effort of climbing up to get a good look had brought Tommy out into a muck-sweat.

'What a climate,' he said as he regained the bridge, and found Morgan Jones there. 'I'm going down to supper.'

'I don't think it'll be ready yet, sir,' said Morgan Jones – 'Number One's only just ordered "carry on cooking".'

'Yet I shall go down,' said Tommy. 'Something tells me that food will soon be ready, and hot.'

He went to the wardroom and ate hugely, after which he stretched himself on his bunk and slept through the night, confident in the ability of his three deck-officers to do all that was necessary . . . Once on patrol there would be little enough rest for the Captain. Tommy possessed that rare gift of being able to lay by a store of sleep in anticipation of shortages to come. Without such a propensity he would long since have cracked up, for he never spared himself when on the job.

In the Petty Officers' Mess Guts Hinton, with his mouth full, was giving the Torpedo Gunner's Mate a direct order.

'I don't care how you feel or what you feel or if you've lost your feeling. *Jimmy-the-One says you're to 'ave a lie in. That's what 'e says and that's what you're goin' to do. Soft-'earted, that's what 'e is.'

Joe Parker was mulish. 'I'll take my trick with the rest,' he said.

'You'll bleeding well do as you're told,' said Guts, forking

*Lower-deck-ese for first-lieutenants.

another spud out of the dish. 'And don't be so finicking proud – not another word! No blasted discipline in this vessel. What do you want?' This to Izzy Sammons.

'My tot,' said the Chief E.R.A.

The coxswain reached across for the bottle and poured out a generous portion. ''Ere you are, Chiefy, I didn't trust your messmates so I kept it back.'

'That's a likely story,' said Izzy, draining his glass at a gulp. 'A likely story indeed.' He smacked his lips. 'Not bad,' he said, 'no water in it this time – what's up, fit o' conscience?'

Guts grinned. 'To think that we're fighting Hitler to save people like you!' He got up, put on his cap and went to the wardroom.

''Alf past eight, sir,' he said. '"Rounds," sir, please,'

Bill Brown yawned. 'Blast!' he said. 'O.K. cox'n.'

They went off together, slaves to the twin gods of routine and discipline, aware that only by complete subservience to them could they hope to endure to the end.

CHAPTER SIX

Half an hour before dawn Tommy was on the bridge and all hands were roused. The traditional hour of surprise was treated with the greatest respect by all submarines; it was never safe to be on the surface at a time of changing visibility, and it was never safe to use one's judgement. The only thing to do was to dive before it began to get light, and this Tommy invariably did, whether he was virtually on the enemy's door-step or, in this case, five hundred miles away from the nearest hostile territory. This time it was no slow-time performance. Tommy simply ordered everybody off the bridge, waited a pause and then following them down the conning-tower hatch, pressed the diving hooter and waited for the engines to stop. Then he shut and clipped the hatch and inserted the safety pins. By the time he had descended the ladder to the control-room the *Gauntlet* was running under with a considerable angle by the bow. In one second Tommy could feel that she was completely under control, and that a good night's rest at sea had got the crew back into their proper form. Everything was going very well, and Tommy's only order was 'Eighty feet', after which he handed the vessel to Bill Brown and went back to the ward-room.

Whilst he turned the pages of an illustrated paper he listened to the goings-on in the control-room and satisfied himself that it was all being done correctly. Then he sat back in his little armchair and, closing his eyes, dropped into another sleep like the good squirrel he was.

An hour later he opened his eyes and stretched himself. Then he went into the control-room and after the usual precautions brought the submarine to thirty feet and looked at the new day through the high-powered periscope.

It was just the same as the previous day, low clouds, continuous rain and breaking seas; and so it would probably be until they returned to harbour. He remembered with regret the blue skies and calm seas of the Mediterranean, which somehow took some of the squalor out of this underwater business. He felt depressed by this continuous downpour and had an urgent desire to go back to his armchair. 'Damnit, I'm getting lazy,' he told himself. 'This won't do.' To his First-Lieutenant he said: 'We'll work up an appetite for breakfast with a spot of gun action.'

'Now, sir?' asked Brown.

'Yes, please.'

'Right! Stand by for gun action!'

The order went throughout the vessel and a 'general post' took place. Men came from the uttermost parts of the submarine and climbed into the conning-tower whilst the three-inch gun's crew did the same thing with the gun access tower, immediately over the wardroom. They were stripped to the waist and carried an assortment of ammunition, machine-guns, gun telescopes and everything necessary for fighting the ship's armament, which consisted of the three-inch gun, the Oerlikon automatic anti-aircraft gun, and two machine-guns. This was an exercise that they all enjoyed, for every man alive is happy when he is able to pull a trigger and make a big bang.

When they were ready Tommy gave them an imaginary target. One round was to be fired from the big gun and bursts of five from the automatics – that was all the ammunition he was prepared to spare. Then he ordered 'Full speed, take her down' and 'Stand by to surface' at the same time.

Down went the submarine's bows and she began to vibrate under the thrust of her propellers. At forty feet on the gauge Tommy ordered the ballast to be blown. The *Gauntlet,* under the momentum of her downward plunge, continued to increase depth for a while, but gradually slowed up until the needles on the gauge hesitated. Then Tommy patted the coxswain on the top of his bald head and that was all that was necessary. Guts spun his wheel to 'hard-a-rise' and so did the second coxswain, and the *Gauntlet* began to rise at a phenomenal speed. By now her ballast tanks were empty and she was as buoyant as a cork.

'Forty!' called Guts.

'Bearing Green four-oh, a target,' ordered Tommy.

'One thousand yards.'

'Thirty!'

'Twenty!'

'Out pins! Off one clip.'

Tommy took a whistle from his pocket and held it to his mouth.

'Ten.'

Tommy blew it. The hatches were flung open and water poured in for a moment, but only for a moment, for nothing would stop the *Gauntlet*'s rush to the surface – up the ladders climbed the guns' crews, and in an incredibly short time the bark of the three-inch gun was followed by a fusillade from the smaller weapons. At the same time both engines started up and the submarine began to shoot ahead at ten knots.

Tommy left the First-Lieutenant to finish off in the control-room and went on to the bridge. The three-inch gun's crew looked thoroughly business-like and pleased with itself, but something was wrong with the Oerlikon. A round was jammed in the breech and would not go either way. Leading Seaman Harrison looked up at his captain.

'It's a different make of ammunition-link, sir – seems a bit tight.' He wrestled with the thing and eventually forced it. Then, inserting another round, he pulled the trigger. A satisfactory burst of five shots followed. Tommy nodded his satisfaction and was thankful that only one round had been a dud. He hoped there were no more.

He dismissed the guns' crews and went down to breakfast.

CHAPTER SEVEN

WITH seven days of the patrol gone by and with absolutely nothing to report, Tommy was beginning to feel guilty. It was no good him telling himself that it wasn't his fault; the facts were there, they might just as well be lying in harbour as patrolling this piece of water. When he had been at the Royal Naval College he had observed a certain practice which the weaker members of a football team were accustomed to observe. On leaving the field at the end of the game they would glance surreptitiously down at their bare knees to see if they were sufficiently muddy. For a cadet to emerge from a game of football with clean knees laid him open to the accusation that he had been skulking. If, therefore, the knees happened to be clean, down he would go, first on one and then on the other, to tighten his bootlaces, at the same time taking the opportunity to repair the deficiency. Tommy was very conscious of his clean knees at this moment, and so was his crew. He must dirty them somehow. Fifteen hundred miles there and back, a month on patrol and nothing to report, was unthinkable. He wondered whether he should take the initiative by going off to a better hunting ground, but reluctantly abandoned the idea. Blind eyes to telescopes were all very well, but his orders were clear-cut, and must be obeyed. Still, he badly needed action, if only for the purpose of taking his own mind off another and more pressing problem. The Gannet was ill and getting no better. Three days out he had spent a wretched night vomiting, and in great pain, which was still there. Everything pointed to appendicitis, that bugbear of all mariners. He lay in his bunk, well doped, and that was pretty nearly all they could do, though instructions in the First Aid book were being followed. If the appendix ceased to be angry, well and good; if it went worse, and ruptured, the Gannet would be buried at sea. Casualties in war are part of the ordinary distressful happenings which must be experienced, but, somehow, a sick man seemed to be outside the rules of this fierce game. If this war was being fought against civilised people, reflected Tommy, he could have found a fishing boat and sent it ashore with the patient, but that was out of the question with these Japanese enemies. A man would rather die among his friends. The effect of having a serious case of illness on board was very lowering to the morale of everybody. It took all the life out of conversation to hear the low and painful coughing of the sick man. People moved on tiptoe and spoke in whispers – there were no occasional bursts of laughter as a joke was served up for the *n*th time. It was almost unbearably hot and humid, and a number of the crew had broken out in rashes which were angry and painful. Altogether this trip was turning out as badly as it could.

During the day Tommy closed the vicinity of Port Blair, the principal defended base of the Andaman group, and worked as close in shore as the depth of water would allow. From there he studied the movements of ships inside the harbour. An occasional patrolling aircraft would force him to lower his periscope, but so far the only surface forces he had seen had been a number of patrol boats, too small to attack with torpedoes, and too heavily armed to risk a surface engagement, for one lucky hit through the hull would have deprived the *Gauntlet* of her cloak of invisibility in a position well within the range of all the enemy aircraft in that part of the Indian Ocean.

During the night Tommy withdrew his command to a position some miles to seaward, and, once there, he surfaced, and gave his crew a chance to breathe, and his electric storage batteries a much needed recharge. The absence of the Gannet from the roster of watch keepers added considerably to Tommy's labours, but that he did not mind. It deprived him of much of his guilty feeling of laziness and took his mind off the dreadful possibility of losing the Sub-Lieutenant. Everybody was fond of Grandison with his coltish ways and gross appetite; among the sailors he was 'subby', a diminutive only used for popular officers. Another point in his favour was that he was by way of being an aristocrat by birth, and would one day (if he lived) succeed to a baronetcy. The ordinary Englishman is very fond of his aristocracy, this inborn snobbishness is there, even amongst the most highly-coloured left-wingers – for there's something about a lord, or even a baronet. At Dartmouth it had been the custom to kick any member of the Royal family, not out of dislike or a sense of disrespect, but simply in order that, at a later date, one might say about the reigning monarch: 'I kicked that chap's backside when he was a kid.' That is a part of the Englishman's character that foreigners will never understand, and is one of the bulwarks against the sort of thing that happens in other countries. The Gannet was an ever-present reminder of the way of life in the homeland, and was popular for that reason. Now he was ill, and everybody was concerned.

Guts Hinton, whose methods consisted of the drastic use of purges, was affronted by Tommy's steadfast refusal to allow him to dose the patient with castor oil. He drew from his store of memories a great number of instances where he had saved life by his ministrations, but Tommy was adamant; he therefore took refuge in the sulks, declaring that 'he'd soon 'ave that scrimshanker on 'is pins again. Fine lookout when a lad of that age takes to his 'mick on a war patrol. Where would we all be if everybody turned in everytime 'e 'ad a bellyache?' To which remarked Izzy Sammons, who was passing at the time, rejoined:

'In bed,' and passed on.

At this stage Morgan Jones announced to his Captain that he was more than two-thirds qualified as a doctor, a fact that hitherto he had kept to himself, for fear of being sent to 'school' again, and made to transfer to the medical branch. Tommy reassured him on this point and felt a bit easier at the thought of having more than half a doctor on board. It took a little of his load off his shoulders.

Bill Brown remained serene through all this welter of inaction. He never changed; a creature of routine he stuck to his task of seeing that the submarine was ready. When the sight and sound of the Gannet's sufferings became too much for him he and Mr Miles would retire to the engine-room and play a few hands of picquet with a pack of aluminium cards which the Chief had fashioned with his own hands.

This, then, was the state of affairs aboard the *Gauntlet* on the morning of the eighth day on patrol. Once more she was close in shore, once more her high-powered periscope was moving lazily through the iron-grey water, turning like the neck of some prehistoric monster, searching for a quarry.

Tommy was eating bacon and eggs without much conviction, when Bill Brown, who had been operating the instrument, stepped quickly into the wardroom.

'Will you come and have a look, sir?' he said. His voice was as matter-of-fact as he could manage to make it, but it was clear that he thought that their luck was changing. Tommy was at the periscope in a matter of seconds.

'What is it?' he asked as he adjusted the focus to his own eyes.

'A smallish steamer,' said Bill, 'about four miles to seaward. Green nine-oh,' he prompted.

'Ah,' said Tommy as he found his target. 'Yes. Smallish, as you say, and but worthy of a brace of fish. Diving stations!'

Bill passed the order and the men off watch went to their stations. Morgan Jones came yawning into the control-room and started to adjust the complicated piece of calculating machinery, used for submarine attacks, known as the fruit-machine. A feeling of business-like relief was apparent. At long last a target had presented itself. Tommy took a lengthy look at it and then snapped up the handles, and nodded to the expectant artificer, who lowered the great instrument into the well.

'Full speed both,' said Tommy, 'eighty feet!'

Guts nodded at Badger and as one man they took the submarine to the ordered depth.

Tommy looked round him and caught Bill's inquiring eye.

'Get all six ready,' he said. 'Targets are few and far between.' It was extravagant to use six torpedoes, but clearly the right policy. He remembered the days of the siege of Malta when it was a matter of a nice calculation to decide when to expend one's irreplaceable stock of torpedoes. The war had moved on a bit since then; torpedoes were plentiful, but targets were scarce – 'in short supply,' as it was said. He grinned with anticipatory delight and all the ennui of the past weeks slipped away. Here was a quarry at last. The stalk was on.

The submarine attack has indeed much in common with deer-stalking, in that the hunter must work himself into a position from which once, and only once, will he be able to fire his shots. Long periods of stealthy approach, running in blind at a great depth, correspond almost exactly to that painful hands-and-knees approach in the wet heather.

Now the *Gauntlet* was going full speed, her electric lights a little dimmer, as the great motors sucked the current with a greed that lowered the voltage of the entire electrical system.

Bill Brown, his eyes everywhere, whispered his orders to Joe Parker in the 'fore-ends', who set about bringing the six bow-tubes to the ready. His voice, mournful and steady, directed the activities of his tubes' crew. In the absence of the Gannet, whose action station should have been forward with the torpedoes, Bill went quickly forward to see if all was well. What he saw satisfied him, and he returned to the control-room. On his way through the wardroom he saw the Gannet's flushed and pain-racked face, peering from behind his bunk curtains.

'What is it?' he asked in a husky whisper.

'A ship at last,' said Bill, 'how are you feeling?'

'A bit better,' lied the Gannet and struggled to a sitting position.

'No you don't, my lad,' said Bill. 'You stay where you are.'

'I'm quite all right, really,' said the Gannet.

'Sure,' said Bill, 'you stay where you are. That's an order.' The Gannet sank back exhausted and Bill passed on.

Tommy was fingering his watch as he studied his attacking instrument. He had been pretty broad on the enemy's bow, and must run in at least two miles to get within effective range, but he dearly wanted to have another look, and to verify his first hasty observations. Moments such as these are a test of any man's patience. He stuffed his watch away and turned his back on the temptation to rise to periscope depth.

The minutes passed and the tension grew. Tommy fingered his chin and hummed a little tune. The crew recognised the symptom and took comfort from it. These moments, rare as they were, were unforgettable. The excitement of the chase, and the almost inevitable retribution which would follow when the enemy counter-attacked, turned the mouth dry and the bowels to water. This was action of the most dangerous sort, but to look at it it seemed to prosaic enough routine.

Presently a whispered report from forward announced

that the torpedo-tubes were ready for firing, barring the final order of 'Stand by', when the safety-pins would be removed. Tommy nodded his acknowledgement and took out his watch.

'Stop both motors,' he ordered. 'Group down.' 'Slow-ahead, port.' Up came the lights as the motors stopped, a faint clang as the giant battery 'grouper' switch connected the batteries in a manner which was more economical for slow speeds, and then the port motor indicating light glowed again.

'Thirty-five,' said Tommy. 'Up periscope.'

Slowly the *Gauntlet* was brought to periscope depth. Tommy stood with his eyes glued to the eyepiece of the periscope waiting for that vital moment when the top window would be clear of the water. What would he see? ... A menacing bow a few yards away? A low-flying aircraft about to drop her bombs? The stern of the target ship which had altered course and run away? Thick fog? Ten minutes 'blind' running is a long time.

'Sixty!' said Guts.

'Fifty!'

'Forty!'

'Level off,' ordered Bill. This was the moment: the submarine must be on an even keel and ready to go straight down again if the Captain decided it. For a few seconds the periscope would be needed. After that another period of blindness would supervene.

'Thirty-six feet,' said Bill and watched his Captain for reactions. Tommy swore a little and polished his eyepieces industriously with tissue paper.

'Where the blazes?' – he said to himself. Then he grunted as he found the target.

'Miles away,' he said mildly. 'Eighty feet! Group up! Full ahead.'

Down went the *Gauntlet* to her depth for running in at full speed. Tommy watched his periscope disappearing into the well and mopped his brow.

'Bigger than I thought,' he said thoughtfully, 'and farther off. Going to be a job to get in.'

Another period of suspense – ten minutes of waiting – and thinking, tinged now by the spectre of disappointed hopes. Tommy always spoke the truth; if he said the chances were small they were small.

It was getting very hot now, for the use of full speed was generating great heat in the batteries and electric motors. Everybody was wet and running with sweat. Shirts, where worn, were saturated, eyeballs pricked saltily, the air was thick and curiously musty.

At last Tommy roused himself. Once more the lights glowed more brightly, once more the *Gauntlet* nosed her way cautiously upwards to periscope depth, once more there was that sickening pause as the Captain's eyes roamed around the surface of the sea. Then came the verdict.

'She's a long shot, but it's worth having a crack.'

A wave of relief went through the control-room. Anything was better than abandoning the attack. As the *Gauntlet* once more hurtled to eighty feet, and sped towards her quarry, spirits became higher. Tommy, in consultation with Morgan Jones, was working out the interval between successive torpedoes so as to 'spread' his salvo of six across the target. At the extreme range at which they were going to be fired the chances of hitting the ship were not very large. A small error in estimation of the enemy's speed, or course, becomes multiplied at great distances. The only way, therefore, to fire at a distant target was to hope for one hit by using long firing-intervals, thus spreading the salvo across the enemy's line of approach. Even as he worked out the details Tommy was aware that his actions were open to criticism. In the Mediteranean he wouldn't have dared to expend his quota of torpedoes on such a doubtful proposition; but here, and with so little signs of enemy activities, he felt that he was justified. After all, torpedoes did find their targets at extreme range, and who knew what the enemy vessel contained? It might be a turning point such as the Staff Officer had envisaged. Anyhow, whatever it was, Tommy's mind was made up.

'Seven seconds interval,' he ordered. 'Out pins!'

There was a pause and then a ghostly voice from forward reported: 'All tubes ready.'

Tommy fingered his watch. He mustn't over-run his time or the target would have passed his line of sight. On the other hand every hundred yards –

'Bring her up,' he ordered. 'Stop both, group down, slow ahead port.'

Curious how there can be forms of silence. The silence of

anticipation of good things to come is completely different from that when the next happening may be a lethal dose of depth-charges. Now, in that control-room, hopes were high. Experience had shown that Tommy seldom bungled any plan which he made.

'Sixty feet,' Guts intoned the depths like an archbishop and gave little warning instructions to the second coxswain by whispers and nodding head.

'Fifty feet!'

'Low power periscope, this time,' said Tommy in that uninterested voice which he always used at decisive moments. 'Up with it!'

The small close-range periscope rose with a hiss, and, as it came up out of the well Tommy seized the handles and slewed the thing round to the angle given by Morgan Jones. He adjusted it with the greatest care, and then, with eyes glued to the eyepieces, stared out, waiting for the dull green water to break away from the top window.

'Forty-feet,' said Guts, adding in a fierce undertone, 'go on, Badger – put some dive on!'

The dull green had gone to a light eau-de-nil, to a clear white, to bubbles and foam, and then, suddenly, to a waste of heaving water, grey and univiting, with small waves which effectively screened the periscope from its target.

'I want to see the target,' said Tommy in a plaintive voice.

'Comin' up, sir,' said Gus reassuringly.

The horizon was getting further away, behind a breaking wave Tommy saw something black – a mast and a wisp of smoke and then suddenly the whole ship.

'Stand by,' he ordered for his sights were nearly on.

Quickly he slewed the periscope right round to see that nothing was likely to come near the *Gauntlet,* and then once more adjusted the instrument to the correct angle of sight. He was just in time. The target's bows were just going to touch the cross-wires. 'Fire!' he ordered, and, as was the custom aboard his ship, everybody repeated the order. A stentorian chorus made certain that those in the torpedo-room would hear the order. An immediate feeling of pressure on the eardrums told these experienced men that the first torpedo had left the tube. This was followed at seven-second intervals by the remainder until the ghostly voice said: 'All torpedoes left the tube.'

Normally, Tommy would have gone to a hundred feet immediately on firing, but the world on the surface seemed so peaceful, with no aircraft, and no escort vessels, and a target some three miles away, that he stayed at periscope depth and watched the enemy.

Would he see a burst of smoke and hear a thunderous noise as evidence of his success? He'd never yet seen the results of his handiwork. People who stayed to watch in the Mediterranean did not always live long enough to regret doing so, but here, as we have said before, was different.

'Seven thousand yards at forty knots,' said Tommy, 'how long does that take?'

'Just over five minutes,' said Morgan Jones.

'That's a very long time,' observed the Captain. In five minutes so much could happen. He watched the target carefully, though now he had fired he had no further control over events. If the enemy altered course, only a little before the five minutes was up, the torpedoes would most probably speed harmlessly by. The silence this time was pregnant with fears of failure.

'Two minutes,' said Morgan Jones.

Bill Brown blew out his cheeks and tried not to look so anxious.

'Three minutes!'

Tommy swore softly.

'Enemy has altered sixty degrees to port.' he said formally. 'I'm afraid that's done it.'

'Four minutes!'

Tommy was certain of his failure and was already debating further action to be taken. The large alteration made by the enemy supply-ship would bring her rapidly closer, but there would not be time to reload the torpedo-tubes before she came up on the *Gauntlet*. There was, however, always the gun.

'Five minutes!'

Not a sound.

'Six minutes!'

Still a hope for the last one to be fired.

'Seven minutes!'

A pall of disappointment settled suddenly on the *Gauntlet*'s crew. Shoulders slumped, men stirred, flexing their limbs, which they had not thought to move since the attack had begun. It was like the movements of a disappointed football crowd after the final whistle. 'Nothin' doing.'

Into this pool of disappointment Tommy threw a brick.

'Gun action stations,' he said.

CHAPTER EIGHT

EVEN as he gave the order, which started the whole grim business, Tommy had a feeling that all was not well. It wasn't usually given to him to hark back, or to indulge in vain regrets, but somehow the sight of the enemy ship, steaming along at a most convenient angle of approach for a torpedo attack, just at the moment when he had expended six of his precious stock of twelve torpedoes, galled him into thinking that on this day he had stepped off with the wrong foot.

If that was the case was it wise to go on with this enterprise? He had only to cancel his last order, to declare that the target had once more altered course and today's particular troubles would be all over.

'There is a tide in the affairs of men' – it was difficult not to think that he'd missed this one. He stared at the approaching vessel through the high-powered periscope and tried hard to see whether this unescorted elderly packet was not in fact an armed Q-boat. Was it wise to risk all by coming to the surface and engaging her on equal terms? – equal, that is, if she had a gun. Had she a gun? He looked a long time at her. There might be something on her poop which could be a gun. A sort of canvas contraption which might be concealing something. One hit from that weapon, and *Gauntlet* would be a mess. Suddenly he was aware that the men in the control-room were looking at him. Had he spoken out loud? if so, what had he said? And what was he thinking of, counting up the risks of a surface engagement? Why, he'd earned a couple of gongs for just this sort of thing. A submarine, properly handled, had all the advantages of surprise. Six quick shots, and down again. The enemy wouldn't have uncovered their gun (if it was a gun) in that time. 'Down periscope,' he ordered.

'Sir?' It was Bill Brown speaking quietly, as usual. 'The Sub wants to take part. Should I let him?'

Tommy turned and saw the Gannet flushed and pleading, binoculars slung over his sweat-soaked pyjamas, eyes bright and feverish.

'Well, Sub,' he said, 'd'you think you're fit enough?'

'I feel quite all right, sir, it'll take my mind off my belly-ache.'

'What do you think, Morgan Jones?'

The Navigator shrugged his shoulders. 'Of course he ought not to, sir,' he said, 'but rightly speaking he ought to be in hospital, but isn't.'

Tommy thought for a moment. The Sub's action station was to be control officer for the three-inch gun. He was a good control officer, calm and unhurried, and he used his head unperturbed by the din of battle. Morgan Jones would have been a poor substitute for him.

'I'll turn in again as soon as we've sunk him,' implored the Gannet.

Tommy grinned with appreciation of the youngster's optimism. 'All right,' he said, 'have a bash if you want to.'

'Oh, thank you, sir.' Here was gratitude indeed.

'O.K. I shall take him on at medium range,' said Tommy. 'I'm not sure whether he's armed. These Japs are not like the Eyeties; they won't panic and hoist the white flag, so we'd better lay off him a bit. I want to fire a dozen rounds. Get on to him as soon as you can and let me know when you're hitting. I may want to alter course after that, but I'll try and make things easy for you.'

'What about the Oerlikon, sir, do you want to open fire with it?' asked the First-Lieutenant.

'No,' said Tommy, 'we may want the ammunition later on.'

He turned to the periscope and nodded at the operator, who brought it smartly out of the well. 'Let's have another look,' he said.

The enemy was closer now. An old black high-funnelled job, burning dirty coal, and flying a tattered ensign; she was steaming at about ten knots, pushing a considerable bow wave ahead of her and rolling heavily in the south-westerly swell. Tommy noted her motion with satisfaction. They'd have to be very good aboard her to lay a gun accurately in that seaway. He decided to modify his plan and to approach the enemy as he surfaced, thus closing the range and making certain of a hit – the *Gauntlet* would make a smaller target, end on; another advantage.

'Down periscope.'

He began to give his preliminary orders in true gunnery style.

'Bearing Green four-oh, an enemy vessel – two masts, one funnel. Range oh-three-five, rate four hundred closing deflection ten left. Open fire on surfacing.'

A comforting ritual this. It took one out of the immediate circumstances and brought to the men, huddled waiting in the access-towers, a sense of gunnery school discipline – it reminded them that somewhere in the world all day and every day someone was giving similar orders, probably a Gunner's mate in gaiters, trying to knock some sense into an Ordinary Seaman's training class. It steadied the nerves to feel the rigid hand of discipline and was a reminder that all that was required of each member of the gun's crew was the correct carrying out of the drill in which he had so often been coached.

'Up periscope!'

A little silence as the Captain, on his hands and knees, caught the handles of the periscope as they emerged from the well and allowed himself to be drawn upwards as he watched for the first breaking of the waves over the top window. Now!

The watchers could see that all was not well but the first order came as a surprise.

'Get the engines ready! Down periscope.'

Tommy turned to Bill Brown and scratched his head. 'The blighter's altered right away,' he said mildly. 'As soon as the engines are ready – we'll surface and chase him. Pass the word. Enemy has altered course.' Then followed fresh gunnery instructions. No sooner were they passed and acknowledged than Mr Miles put his head through the engine-room doorway and reported: 'Engines ready!'

'Right,' said Tommy. 'Fifty feet, cox'n, stand by to surface!'

A sigh of relief was almost audible. The time had come. Action at last.

Tommy watched the needles of the depth gauges and carried out the drill so often practised on the way to Port Blair. Scarcely a word was necessary. He nodded to Bill when he wanted the tanks to be blown, he patted Guts's bald pate at the moment when the planes should be reversed.

He took the whistle from its hook in the control-room and gave three separate orders.

'Of one clip!'

'Stand by.'

The depth gauge pointers were winding back at ever-increasing speeds.

'Thirty feet!' called Guts.

'Twenty feet!'

Tommy put the whistle to his lips.

'Ten feet!'

Tommy blew it.

Slam – bang! went the hatches and down came a refreshing, but temporary, cascade of water. The men cheered as they went up through it like salmon leaping the rapids. All was noise, bustle and purposeful action.

Tommy swung the engine telegraphs to 'Full Ahead' and clambered rapidly up the conning-tower ladder on the heels of the last of the gun's crew. As he reached the air the three-inch gun began to talk. Bang! Bang! Bang! Rapid fire indeed. But where were the shots going?

Tommy climbed up on the periscope standard in time to see a shot sending up a tall gout of spray close to the starboard side of the enemy.

'Left eight!' came the steady voice of the Gannet. 'Fire!'

Bang again!

'Right four!' went on the Sub. 'Fire.' Bang again.

Tommy waited for the shot to fall but before it did he saw the Japanese ship turning under full helm.

'Enemy altering course,' he yelled and jumped to the voice-pipe. This was an unexpected turn of events. If the enemy came straight for him he must either turn away or dive, or both, and that quickly.

'Hard a-starboard,' he ordered. From the other end of the pipe his order was repeated. Quickly the *Gauntlet* swung to starboard.

'Check! Check!' ordered the Sub. It was clearly impossible to train the gun with sufficient accuracy, as the submarine was swinging under full helm. 'Gun won't bear!' he reported.

'Open fire with the Oerlikon,' ordered Tommy, for this gun was mounted behind the bridge.

He went to the voice-pipe again as the Oerlikon began to beat a tattoo. 'Midships!' he ordered. 'Steady as you go!'

Then things began to go wrong. The Oerlikon ceased firing and at the same moment the first shot from the enemy threw a great plume of water over the bridge. She was indeed armed and coming in to attack. Tommy took a quick decision. It was his duty to break off the action and to get under water as quickly as possible.

'Oerlikon jammed, sir!'

'Down below everybody,' said Tommy. 'Stand by to dive' – this down the voice-pipe.

'Helm jammed, sir.'

It was indeed! *Gauntlet* was still swinging towards the rapidly approaching target.

'Hand steering,' came the faint echo of the order through the voice-pipe. The last man was just disappearing down the gun-tower hatch. 'Hurry up!' said Tommy. He'd not known a worse situation. He must get under water. He leant down to press the klaxon switch, when a swoosh, a roar, a flash and a dull bang sent him reeling. A puff of smoke came out of the bridge voice-pipe, followed by Bill Brown's steady voice.

'We've been hit, sir, on the water line. Water coming in I'm sending the gun's crew on deck again.'

'Right,' said Tommy. 'Get that steering gear working.' He lifted his voice. 'Get a move on the gun's crew. You can't miss him at this range.'

Which was only too true. Desperately the men clambered up and swung the gun on to its bearing.

'Twelve rounds rapid!' ordered the Sub. The gun banged away. Now the enemy were not more than a mile away. Three shots had screamed overhead. The next one would hit for certain. It arrived with a roar and a shriek and burst in the casing, sending wicked splinters in all directions.

Tommy saw a Leading Seaman fall across his sights and the Gannet pulling him back with an extraordinary feat of strength.

'Helm in hand,' came the voice from below. 'Thank God!'

'Hard a-port,' ordered Tommy. Another shell burst in the casing farther forward. The Jap shooting was getting wild.

'We've hit him, sir,' the signalman reported. 'Twice! No, three times!'

The Gannet was making good shooting at last, laying his own gun and ordering corrections to the sight-setter in a steady voice. Now the two vessels were broadside on at a range of a mile, and for the first time since the action had begun, the enemy was taking punishment. The Gannet, having established a hitting range, was ordering the trainer to get on the enemy's single gun which had done so much damage.

Three more shots and a great cloud of soot shot up from the enemy's funnel, she began to list and her speed fell off.

'Finish her off,' said Tommy.

The navigator touched him on the arm. 'Look, sir,' he said, 'a submarine chaser!'

Once again Tommy made a convulsive gesture towards the diving hooter and then, recollecting what the First-Lieutenant had said, went to the voice-pipe.

'Ask the First-Lieutenant how he's getting on,' he said.

A few seconds later Bill appeared in the conning-tower hatch. 'Water's coming in pretty fast, sir,' he said. 'We must try and plug it from outside.'

'No question of diving?'

Bill shook his head.

'There's a Jap submarine chaser after us,' said Tommy.

Bill went white.

'Do your best!' said Tommy. 'We're doing wonders with the three-inch.' He shouted at the Oerlikon's crew who were feverishly stripping their useless weapon. 'Get a move on,' he said, 'we shall need that!' Down the voice-pipe again he conned the submarine to run away from his enemy and from the approaching submarine chaser. The only hope now lay in flight, and what a hope!

CHAPTER NINE

When Petty Officer Telegraphist Bert Toogood heard the order for gun action stations he roused himself from his motionless vigil in the wireless cabinet, and made certain adjustments to his receiving set. Once on the surface he might intercept a message from headquarters, or beyond. Sitting day after day in a submerged submarine gave one a feeling of complete isolation, and this break on the surface would be welcome in spite of the hazards which went with it.

Tommy had not been entirely right when he had prophesied that Bert would never have a repetition of the dream that he had described. The dream had come back frequently, but now Bert had a plan ready for dealing with the situation. Many of his waking hours had been devoted to possible means of stopping that everlasting gush of incoming water, most of them fantastically impossible; nevertheless, they had the effect of lessening the horror which the nightmare used to bring, until now the dream, if not welcome, had the familiarity of an old enemy and was completely divorced from the real thing.

Bert's office was on the lower 'floor' at the after end of the control-room and had a short voice-pipe to that compartment, so that although he could see nothing, what he could hear kept him completely informed. Action on surface, in his experience, was usually a one-sided affair with some wretched little supply ship caught napping, and turned, in a few seconds, into a smoking charnel-house. It was war, but it was not magnificent, and it was hardly dangerous. That being the case the interception of outside signals was of first importance, and so, as the excitement and bustle overhead indicated that surface action was imminent, Bert tuned his aerial and as soon as the *Gauntlet* broke surface concentrated on listening for news from another world. As the first bang of the three-inch gun sounded dully overhead he heard *Carpentaria* broadcasting at one of her stated routine times. It wasn't a very long signal, but it covered a whole page of paper with five-letter 'groups' which must be decyphered. The *Carpentaria* broadcast the same signal twice and then went off the air. Bert was agog to see the import of the message, and worked on the decyphering of it, whilst the world up top rattled and banged. So concentrated was he on his work that he missed the order to stand by to dive again. When, however, he had got half-way through the message, and saw that it was not of any apparent import to him, or anyone aboard, being information concerning the movements of another submarine – the *Goose* – his interest began to flag, and he became aware for the first time that all was not well up top. With half an ear to the outside world, he copied the signal neatly into his signal log, and stuck the original on a sharp-pointed file. Then he shifted his ear a bit nearer the voice-pipe. It was difficult to size up the situation, but anyone would know that things were difficult, the steering gear had jammed to start with – the guns had ceased firing for a while, the First-Lieutenant was getting things under control from a state of confusion most unusual in the *Gauntlet*. Everything seemed to be a bit hay-wire, and not at all as it used to be in those sudden surface butcheries, back in the days of the 'Med.' What had happened to cause all this? In answer to his question came a mighty bang which put his lights out in the cabinet. There was a smell of high explosive and the sound of rushing water. But he didn't feel particularly afraid; only curious to see how it matched his dream. Methodically he turned on the secondary lighting, and tidied up the desk of his office; then he felt his feet were wet and looking down saw water rising rapidly above the door.

He opened his sound-proof door and the whole grim reality of the situation burst upon him. A large amount of water was pouring in through a hole in the *Gauntlet*'s hull, high up under the after end of the conning-tower, as far as one could judge. It was not coming in under any great pressure, but rather with the persistence with which water runs out of a bath. In addition to this, splinters from the explosion had perforated some oil pipes which were squirting vigorously all over the place. Already the water had nearly filled the cavities containing the wireless and Asdic offices. Soon it would slop over the sill of the engine-room doorway. No one seemed to be doing very much for the moment. Bill Brown, though calm, was more concerned with getting the steering gear going, than stopping the water from coming in – though Bert heard him order all pumps to be put on the after bilges. He also heard a voice reporting that the bilge pumps were out of action as they were already submerged by the inrush of water. Not only that but all the lighting fuses had blown.

To the one man who had not in any way been shocked by the build-up of this disaster there seemed only one thing to do – stop the water from coming in, *or perish.*

Bert pushed his way forward, past white-faced men who were getting used to the idea of having only a few more minutes to live, went to his bunk, and caught up a roll of blankets and started back to the control-room. At the door he nearly collided with his assistant, whose action station had taken him to be part of the ammunition supply party.

'What do you think you're doing?' asked the Leading Telegraphist.

'I'm going to bung the 'ole up,' said Bert, 'Come on, Sparko.'

Sparko looked doubtfully round and then decided to follow his chief. Together they struggled past the men in the control-room, climbing the ladder, crept unobserved on to the bridge and started to climb over the back end of it, clutching their blankets as if they were precious babies.

'What are you doing?' demanded Tommy.

'Pluggin' the 'ole,' said Bert simply and dropped out of sight.

Tommy was far too exercised to follow this up, he was watching the submarine chaser and thinking to himself that something akin to a miracle was necessary to extract him from his present predicament. At that moment the first favourable development occurred. A direct hit on the enemy's gun from the Oerlikon, which had consented to fire again for a while, had a remarkable effect. The wounded ship slowed down and turned away, and what was even better the submarine chaser made a large alteration of course and went to the aid of his consort. For the moment the *Gauntlet* was free to lick her wounds.

Down on the pressure hull Bert and Sparko were pressing a blanket down through the swirling water into a jagged hole, through which the interior of the submarine was occasionally visible; but little success attended their efforts.

The *Gauntlet* was going too fast. They had to hold on with all their strength to avoid being swept away by the rush of water past the submarine's hull and had little left for any successful plugging operation.

''Ang on where you are,' said Bert. 'I'm going to talk to the Skipper.' He climbed back and touched his forelock to Tommy. 'If you could ease her down for a bit we could stop the 'ole up,' he said.

'Um,' said Tommy, 'is it a large hole?'

'Yes, sir,' said the First-Lieutenant who had come up at that moment. 'The engine-room's got a lot of water in it.'

Tommy looked at the submarine chaser only two miles away. He was most reluctant to stop engines, but it was clear that he must.

'All right,' he said. 'Quick as you like.'

Down went Bert as the telegraphs were put to 'stop'. The two men set about the plugging operation with more method this time. A tight roll of blanket was seized with a bit of lashing and packed into the centre of the jagged hole in the hull. Then strips of material were rolled up and forced into the remaining crevices. Bill Brown leaned over the bridge and watched them working, wondering as he did so whether he'd given any orders to do this or whether Toogood had taken it on himself to do it. He must find out when it was all over.

Tommy was dancing with impatience now. 'How are they getting on?' he demanded.

'Nearly finished now,' said Bill, 'I'll go down and see how things are going. We'll have to get this water out with buckets; the bilge pumps are under water, and the hand one in the engine-room can't cope.'

'All right,' said Tommy, 'what's the matter with the steering gear?'

'The pressure piping got hit. We shall have to steer from aft.'

'Submarine chaser's coming this way, sir,' reported the signalman, and as he spoke a plume of water rose a few feet to port of the bridge and a burst of yellow flame shot along the surface of the water.

'Open fire,' ordered Tommy. He leaned over the bridge taffrail and shouted at Bert. 'I'm going ahead now. Hold on.'

Bert was too dazed to hear what he said. He was examining his feet. A few seconds before he had had on a pair of boots, properly laced up. Now, his feet were bare and tingling as if they had been placed in a bath of acid. He looked up and saw Sparko looking at him anxiously.

'Blown me boots off,' he said. 'I reckon that's a bit thick, that is.'

'Skipper says we're going ahead,' shouted Sparko, 'better get up on the bridge or we'll be washed off. Come on.'

Another shot fell astern, and another. Then the submarine chaser turned again and went to the aid of the larger vessel now perilously near sinking. Tommy watched the two vessels getting smaller every minute and was amazed that they had let him escape. But he was under no illusions about what would happen next, and began to make fresh plans to face the inevitable air attack.

Meantime Bill had collected a surprising number of buckets, and had placed men at intervals from the after end of the control-room, up the conning-tower, to the bridge. The blanket plug had greatly reduced the inflow, but even so, it was coming in as fast as a bucket chain could handle it. At this moment the *Gauntlet* could not be classified as a good risk, and there was much worse to come. They had got away from the surface vessels, but soon the aircraft would arrive in force.

Tommy looked at his watch and could not believe that is was only nine in the morning. Nine hours' more daylight – what chances had they of surviving for that length of time!

CHAPTER TEN

Now that the first reaction to the sudden catastrophe had resolved itself into a grim determination to stay alive, every man turned to the task nearest him. Where he was not under direct orders he looked around to see how he could help. Here were the fruits of long association in the bonds of comradeship far closer than any discipline could have enforced among disciplined men.

Guts Hinton no longer had any duty to perform at surface action stations, and, since diving was out of the question, he set about dealing with the wounded. Here was an opportunity to practise the skill which he had acquired in first-aid courses. He had long planned a suitable layout for hospitalising part of the submarine. Now he set about putting it into action as calmly as if it did not involve getting far away from any means of escape should the submarine founder. In times of danger it requires a very brave man to remove himself from the only hope of survival, should the worst occur. There was far too much of a crowd gathering in or near the forward control-room door; Guts's first job was to send it packing.

'Wot's your job?' he asked one of the torpedo hands (as if he didn't know!)

'I came to see if I could help,' said the man.

'Well, you can,' said the coxswain, 'come on.' He walked right forward to where Joe Parker and his other fore-end-man were busy preparing a torpedo for loading into the now empty tubes. It was quiet forward and the knowledge that the submarine was quietly flooding amid-ships gave a tomb-like quality to the silence. Joe Parker and his mate were working with little conversation when Guts arrived, but after a few minutes listening to his considerable powers of rhetoric and reinforced by the missing hand, they were once again reloading the torpedo tubes at full speed.

Guts watched them for a moment and then turned to a

couple of stokers, whose duties had brought them forward to help pass ammunition from the magazine to the gun access trunk. Bidding them redouble their efforts to get a healthy supply of ammunition in the form of a dump at the foot of the tower, he stood over them until they moved as fast as Keystone Cops, and when they returned panting and dripping with sweat, he switched them into the torpedo-room to help with the hand-loading gear, for by now the hydraulic system had failed. Backwards and forwards he rampaged, whipping up the flagging spirits of the men trapped below until they had no time to think of their predicament. Then, when the last torpedo disappeared into the last tube, he had them down on their hands and knees, swilling and swabbing until the torpedo-room, now empty, was shining as if for an inspection. Next he had half a dozen frame-cots taken from the messes (mostly, I regret to report, from the Artificers' mess) and fixed with lashings in the racks where, hitherto, had lain the torpedoes. When they were nearly fixed he collected his stokers and with a stretcher, specially designed for handling casualties in a vertical position, he set out in search of patients for his hospital.

He found three likely ones. The gunlayer was slumped down over the ready-use ammunition lockers, bleeding profusely from a gash in the neck. Someone had already bandaged it, with little effect: a large vein was cut and the man was bleeding to death. They did their best to get him below and into a cot, but he was dead before they got him there. Guts, apparently unmoved by this check to his plans, covered the poor thing with a blanket, and set out with a fresh determination. His next attempt to capture a patient was concentrated on the Sub-Lieutenant, who told him to go to hell. He then heard of Toogood's feet, and this time got a customer, applying a picric acid dressing to the burns with great skill. Toogood waited until his feet were done, then he thrust them into an old pair of carpet slippers and went back to look at his plug.

In the control-room the bucket chain was beginning to settle down to its endless task. Men had discovered where to stand, how to economise in physical effort, how to avoid spilling too much of the contents, and how to pass back the empties in a sort of rhythm. The watching First-Lieutenant, counting the flow of buckets, calculated that he was getting water *out* of the *Gauntlet* at the rate of twenty gallons a minute. It appeared to be coming in at slightly more than that speed. They would nearly be able to hold their own, until they were exhausted, or unless something dislodged the plug. Two things were necessary, therefore, to improve the situation: one was to get a pump going, and thus relieve at least some of the hard labour of the bucket chain; the other was to fix a more efficient sealing-device on the outside of the submarine. With the first of these aims in view, he clambered past the bailers, and splashed through the little brook which was cascading into the engine-room, over the sill of the doorway which had to be kept open in order to give the engines a supply of air, without which the Diesels could not function.

Conditions in the engine-room were frightfully bad. The bilges were full and water was two feet over the foot-plates in the gangway. All the electric machinery was already submerged and out of action, except by some miracle of good fortune the circulating pumps, which some blessed designer had arranged to be high up in the engine-room. If the circulaters packed up so did the engines; with the engines went their last hope of survival. Mr Miles stood on the little raised platform at the back-end of the engine-room. His pipe was in his mouth, more as an act of bravado than anything else. He was very frightened – he had far too much knowledge of the situation to be otherwise. At any moment one or both of his engines might stop. It was impossible to tell where the water, which was now swirling into the crank-pits, would get to, and it could only be a matter of time before it found its way into the main motors which were not separated by a water-tight bulkhead from the engines. Mr Miles was facing the fact that his wife was shortly going to become a widow. It distressed him, but he had faced it. He saw Bill Brown and gave him the sort of nod that a business man gives to an associate on a wet Monday morning; it signified the epithet 'Bloody?' Bill gave him back a similar nod and went into the motor compartment.

One of the operators was looking at an earth-lamp which was glowing brightly as an indication that the main motor insulation was broken down to zero. One of the electric motors was thus already out of commission. The other would no doubt follow suit. He instructed the man to draw all the fuses and went forward again with heavy heart, and some really bad news for the Captain. From now on the

Gauntlet was living on capital as far as electricity was concerned. With the electric motors out of action there was no means of recharging the submarine's batteries, so that when they were run down that would be the end. No light, and no current for the circulating pumps.

As he waded back through the engine-room the starboard engine began to scream and judder. Mr Miles flung himself upon the control-levers and stopped the thing before it disintegrated. Then he turned to Bill and shouted: 'Tell the Skipper starboard engine stopped!'

'What's the matter with it?' asked Bill.

'Piston seized, number eight cylinder.'

'Can't you do anything?'

'I'll try.'

'O.K.' Bill went on. As he entered the control-room he heard his name down the voice-pipe. The Skipper wanted to speak to him urgently. Bill forced his way past the bucket-chain and reached the bridge.

Tommy was searching the sky with his glasses. He spoke but did not interrupt his vigil.

'What's it like below, Number One?' he asked.

'Pretty bad,' said Bill. 'The starboard motor has a dead earth and I've drawn the fuses of both. The starboard engine has siezed. The wireless office is flooded and all the pumps are out of action.'

Tommy kept his eyes to his glasses.

'We can expect air attack at any moment,' he said. 'We'd better concentrate on defending ourselves. If we can hold on until darkness we might be able to get some repairs under way. Get every spare hand on to ensuring a good ammunition supply, and *keep the buckets going.*'

Bill looked round the horizon; far away astern were the squat hulls of their enemies. From their inability to administer the *coup de grâce* there arose the faint hope that perhaps the Japanese air force was equally inefficient. Certainly they were a long time coming.

'By the way,' said Tommy, 'what's the matter with the gyro-compass?'

'Splinter through the pressure-casing,' said Bill.

'How are they managing aft,' asked the Captain, 'with no repeater to steer by?'

'I'll go and see,' said Bill. He'd forgotten about those heroes in the after compartment struggling with an almost unmanageable hand-steering wheel.

Quickly he went down aft, through the line of buckets, over the waterfall, into the engine-room where the water surged into fierce little waves in the uneasy rolling of the submarine. She was losing buoyancy with all this weight of water. He must blow every drop of internal ballast except the drinking water. He stopped and shouted his instructions in the Chief's ear and went on his way. There in the extreme after end two men were trying to steer a course by a small magnetic compass which was far too close to the steel structure, and electrical devices in the compartment, to be anything but utterly unreliable. As he opened his mouth to speak to the two sweat-sodden men who wrestled grimly with their task, an order came faintly through the control-room voice-pipe. 'Hard-a-starboard!' And at the same moment the submarine quivered under the recoils of all her gun armament. The air attack had begun.

Bill's imagination was not under-developed. As he crouched aft he could see the Japanese bombers coming in in headlong cascades, their machine-guns ablaze and their bomb-aimers ready. An almost irresistible urge to get out of this rat-trap to God's fresh air, before it was too late, had to be conquered by a great effort of will. He saw the two men eyeing him, and laid a hand on a spare spoke of the steering wheel.

'Come on, chaps,' he said quietly, 'let's work the helm as fast as we can. The Skipper will be wanting to dodge those bastards.'

The three pairs of hands laid together on the same object saved each man from taking flight.

'Midships' came another faint order. They sweated on the wheel and orders came thick and fast. A series of nasty crumps now accompanied the joltings of the submarine's own guns; as far as one could judge from down below they were not particularly near misses. Presently there was a lull. Bill Brown gave a grin at the two men and said: 'Looks as if we've come through that all right. O.K.?'

The older member nodded. 'O.K., sir,' he said. He had no illusions about the situation. He was grateful for the company of the First-Lieutenant and sorry to be left.

'I'll come back and see how you're getting on,' said Bill, and went on his way.

CHAPTER ELEVEN

'AIRCRAFT in sight, bearing red one-seven-oh!'

It had come at last. Tommy got down from his pedestal by the big periscope, and looked at his defence preparations. They were as ready as they could be. The three-inch, with the Gannet, flushed and fever-eyed, as layer, was waiting on the extreme after-bearing possible, its muzzle cocked up in a pathetic attempt to turn itself into an anti-aircraft weapon, which it certainly was not. Abaft the bridge, the Oerlikon, black, lean, and wicked looking, was already laid on the approaching enemy, a flight of four medium bombers by the look of them. On the after end of the bridge the two machine-gunners were waiting for their chance. Itching fingers were all very well, but the ammunition supply was strictly limited.

'Do *not* open fire, until I give the order,' said Tommy, 'and when you do fire don't waste the stuff.'

'Stand by everybody! They're coming in now!'

It wasn't a pleasant thing to see the bombers peeling off and coming in as if on a practice run, and to do nothing to put them off their stroke, but Tommy had decided that this battle was likely to be one of attrition, *if they were not destroyed outright by a direct hit*. He had some experience, and had heard a lot, of the charmed life which submarines could bear under repeated air attacks. The problem was a simple one. A direct hit would finish them, darkness would give them respite. Avoiding action and gun-fire might keep the attackers at a safer distance.

The first one was coming in.

'Hold it,' said Tommy and then down the voice-pipe, 'Hard-a-starboard!'

The black, ugly, squat-looking bomber was getting bigger every minute. As *Gauntlet* swung under full helm Tommy gave the order 'Open fire'. The response was most impressive and comforting. The bomber was obviously not expecting such a reception. It waggled its wings like a live thing, as if the pilot had received a great surprise. Then it came down upon them, its machine-gun blazing. Tommy crouched for protection behind thin brass sheeting and watched a furrow of bullets narrowly miss the bridge. At the same moment he saw two bombs leave the aircraft and felt the draught from the machine's propellers as it passed, a few feet overhead. 'Far too near for the bombs to arm before hitting,' he thought, and was right. One of them landed on the casing and bounced into the sea without exploding, the other narrowly missed and exploded at a considerable depth, well astern. The machine itself made a desperate effort to pull out from its dive. It reared up on its tail, flames coming out of the port engine, then it stalled, side-slipped, and crashed in flames, a heartening sight indeed. For the first time since everything had gone wrong Tommy wondered if, after all, there was not still some faint hope.

No time for cheering. The second bomber was coming in. Down it came, in imitation of the first, but the fate of its predecessor made it more cautious, while Tommy's frantic helm alterations made a steady run-in an impossibility. Two more bombs fell at a safe distance. The bomber rose steeply and flew round for another run-in.

Number three was made of sterner stuff. He made a good run-in, dropped his bombs at the right moment, swerved violently to put off the machine-gun fire and zoomed up overhead just as they exploded. There were two tremendous crumps, smoke and flame was everywhere – there was the thud and a cry of a hit man, and the clang of tortured steel as splinters flew. The attacking plane went unscathed away and Tommy saw that its aim had been too good. As the last of the four came in the Oerlikon was silent – so was the three-inch. Only the two bridge guns answered. The bombs dropped close alongside, so close that it felt as if the *Gauntlet* had been hit.

Tommy went to the voice-pipe. 'Are you there, Number One?'

There was no reply for a moment. Then a faint and anxious voice replied. 'First-Lieutenant's comin' now, sir.'

It was followed by the most welcome and almost hearty voice of Bill Brown himself.

'First-Lieutenant here, sir.'

'All right below?'

A pause as Bill looked round. 'Nothing serious – extra – that was pretty close.'

'It was,' said Tommy. 'Come up and sort things out. We're in a bit of a mess up here. And send up the stretcher party!'

CHAPTER TWELVE

As he worked his way up the conning-tower, past the bucket party, sweating and swearing, but still joking desperately, Bill Brown remembered a picture he'd once seen of a flying-fish pursued under water by some shoal of voracious marauders and in a frantic effort to escape them, jumping into the beak of a waiting sea-bird. He felt very much like the fish. Down below he was in a wet and half-lit tomb with the menace of the encroaching water urging him to reach the open air at all costs; surely it was better to fight a clean fight in one's own element, rather than wait for a protracted end beneath the surface?

The men on the bridge, however, weren't liking it at all. They had no protection against the bullets, bombs and splinters and the sight of enemy aircraft diving in, all guns ablaze, was frankly terrifying. Bill's arrival coincided with a sudden return attack by one of the early aircraft. He saw the spray of bullets cutting a swath across the upper deck and miraculously missing everybody and he watched the bombs tumbling from under the machine and he was afraid. He wanted to bolt into the security of an inch of steel-plating, but compromised by withdrawing his head into the open hatch-way like a frightened tortoise. As the bombs reached the sea Tommy ordered: 'Down everybody!' and everybody went down, cowering as best they could and with as much cover as a partridge in stubble.

The bombs exploded. Sundry splinters whizzed overhead; others hit the submarine's casing with terrifying force. The prostrate men rose slowly and each one looked to see who was not able to do so. By one of those miracles which happen every minute of every day in times of battle, no one was touched.

Tommy saw Bill and called him to come and talk. There was nothing to do now but make a last ditch stand. With eight hours of daylight and manoeuvring only on one engine, it would be impossible to escape from the enemy air force, who would be free to enjoy their target practice until they had scored a direct hit. This, according to the law of averages, could only be a matter of time, but Tommy knew, and so did all his veteran crew, that averages didn't work like that; if they did there was no point in making those desperate efforts to postpone the inevitable. There was a real fighting chance, if nothing went very much further wrong. There were three points which must be consolidated. Firstly, the submarine must be kept afloat. Already it was easy to see that she was floating some eighteen inches below her surface trim. The hole in the hull was now under constant pressure, and water was forcing its way past the blanket-plug at an increasing rate. Something better must be done with that. Bert Toogood had shown the way, since but for his quick reactions they would not be afloat now.

'Something more permanent,' said Tommy, 'get the Chief on to it. Tell him to cut a piece of casing away and make a sealing plate.' His eyes roamed round the bridge and saw the little metal chart table. 'The very thing!' he said.

Secondly, the guns' crews must be kept up to strength and that infernal Oerlikon persuaded to fire.

Thirdly, the engine must be kept going. He recounted his points on his fingers. 'Nothing else matters,' he said. 'If we can hang on until dark we'll think again. Now get going.'

'Aircraft, red one-five-oh!'

Bill ran to the three-inch gun, whose trainer had a nasty gash and was bleeding profusely. Bill took the wheel while the loading numbers helped the wounded man down the hatch-way to the waiting arms of Guts Hinton. It was good to feel a wheel in one's hands and to look over the sights at the approaching enemy. Anything was better than doing nothing.

The single aircraft came in at a respectable height. Tommy waited for the right moment and then, with the use of extreme rudder made a violent swerve. The bombs dropped very wide and little or no ammunition was expended by the defence.

Bill reluctantly turned over his wheel to the second coxswain and went to the Oerlikon's crew, who had dismantled their gun and were fitting the spare barrel. There was nothing to do here, they were working as fast as human beings could.

He looked down on to the casing and was surprised to see Bert Toogood still there, jabbing down at his plug with a broomstick. He looked worried and he was pushing with all his might.

'If I don't hold,' he said, 'it'll work out.'

'Well, hold it then,' said Bill, 'but don't fall over the side.'

Bert gritted his teeth and pushed with the stick down into the swirling water.

'How are your poor old feet?' asked Bill.

'O.K. sir.'

Bill went back to the Captain. 'Toogood's on the casing, sir, and it's getting a bit lively there. I'm afraid he might go over the side.'

'Put a line on him,' said Tommy. 'Here comes another one. Hard-a-starboard!'

In came the enemy, guns blazing. The three-inch gun gave a few perfunctory barks, the machine-guns rattled in satisfactory manner, and the men at the Oerlikon, performing superhuman feats of strength, finished and were able to fire one round at the plane before it swept by, leaving its bombs as ill-aimed mementoes to explode harmlessly some distance away.

There was no doubt, thought Bill, as he went down into the dark and dripping interior of the submarine, that these Japs were not of county-cricket standard. At the bottom of the hatch Guts Hinton was waiting.

' 'Ow are we doing, sir?' he asked.

'If those bloody Nips don't score a lucky one,' Bill said, 'we may get away with this.'

Guts didn't react the way that he should.

'What's the matter?' asked Bill with a grin. 'Aren't you happy in your work?'

'It's that Mr Jones, what's he doing messing around the wounded? I'm the proper one to do that.'

'Hell,' said Bill, 'I forgot to tell you – Mr Morgan Jones is practically a fully qualified doctor. The Skipper's put him in charge of the wounded. Sorry, cox'n, I forgot to tell you.'

'Oh, it's of no account to me, I'm sure,' said the coxswain. 'I just like to – ' A large explosion drowned his final words and he went forward the very picture of affronted pride. If he were blotted out that moment he would take his grievance with him to Valhalla and go on with the argument there. As it was he went back to his 'hospital' with less enthusiasm. One of the men with a superficial cut on his arm greeted him anxiously.

''Ow are we doing, 'Swain?' he asked.

'Don't know and don't care,' said Guts – 'I just like to know where I stand.'

'Well, stand out of the way,' said Morgan Jones, advancing with an armful of bandages. 'Are these all we've got?'

Guts pulled himself together. He had no opinion of any reserve officers, and had always begrudged the respect that he had shown to the Navigator. Now the man had turned out to be a doctor. 'Them's all we're allowed.'

'It's not going to be enough,' said Morgan Jones. 'Round up all the shirts and handkerchiefs you can find, and look lively.'

Guts recoiled for a moment at the incisive order and then his training came to his rescue, 'Aye, aye, sir!' he said and lumbered away.

Down aft Bill was shouting above the din of the engine into Mr Miles's ear. 'A patch,' he was saying, 'two feet square. The bridge chart table would do.'

Mr Miles nodded. 'I'll send Izzy up,' he said, 'he's clever with his hands.' He put two fingers in his mouth and a whistling noise of extraordinary quality cut through the din of the Diesels, like a knife, to reach the ears of the little Chief Engine-room Artificer who came splashing through two feet of water without showing undue excitement.

'What is it?' he said.

Mr Miles bent to his ear. 'Go up with Number One and he'll show you what he wants,' he said. 'A patch to put over the hole.'

'Just a minute,' said Izzy. He moved back through the swirling water and gave some final instructions to a gang he'd collected. Then he waded along and joined Bill in the control-room.

'Reckon those buckets want improving on,' he said. 'I've got the spare circulating pump to play with. When we've disconnected it and fitted a suction to the bilge it'll pull the water quicker than kiss-your-'and.' He looked up at the cascading leak in the hull. 'Now, what about this patch?' he asked.

Bill explained the situation. Something soft to seat it on was required and something to hold it down. Izzy listened and his eyes roamed around as he took in the requirements.

Then he went quickly aft and slashed his way back to the engine-room, as if it was normal to walk about up to the knees in water. 'Get me tools,' he said over his shoulder.

'Just like a bloody plumber,' said Guts. 'Excuse me, sir, but Mr Jones wants all your clean 'ankies and shirts, for bandages; shall I take 'em?'

'Of course,' said Bill. He felt much better with all this wealth of improvisation. This was no case of a few despairing efforts. Everybody was pulling his weight. 'Pray God the Nips don't hit us,' he said to himself, 'we'll pull through if they don't, I'll swear we will.'

Though how this was to be accomplished he'd so far no idea at all. And at that moment the only man aboard who could save the ship was in imminent peril of drowning. Bert Toogood, not content with holding the plug in with his broomstick, had gone down to tread it in at the same moment as Tommy put his helm hard over as yet another aircraft bore down upon them. The *Gauntlet*, laden with loose water swilling in her compartments, lurched heavily; a green sea swept along her casing and plucking up Bert Toogood, pitched him on his side so that before he could hold on afresh he was struggling in the creamy wake astern.

'Man overboard!' It was one of the Oerlikon's crew who saw it happen. Tommy jumped down and sized up the situation. With one propeller working and no astern power (for normally the electric motors provided that) there was only one hope – to continue the circle he had begun in the hope of finishing up within reach of Toogood on its completion. Meanwhile the enemy aircraft approached. It was a vicious attack, and provided two more patients for the hospital, but no bombs were dropped, thus saving Toogood's life; for their concussion, at such close range, would have finished him off. Some success attended the machine-gunners' efforts; as the aircraft went away a shower of splinters from a damaged propeller tore the surface of its starboard plane. Flames were seen to be spouting from its engine exhaust. It lost a little height and flew away with a heavy list, much to the encouragement of the men on deck. Tommy jumped up on to the periscope for-and-after and watched Toogood. Meanwhile the wardroom Flunkey removed all his clothes and provided himself with a light line and a life-buoy. No one questioned his act. Bert Davis was known to be a first-class water polo player, and champion breast-stroke swimmer of the Mediterranean Fleet. He was clearly the man for rescue work of this kind. It was typical of the unity of this submarine's crew that no words passed as the rescuer clambered down on to the casing, ready for the moment to dive in with a line as he had so often done before when recovering practice torpedoes.

The *Gauntlet* turned steadily as long as the engine was kept going ahead, but when, as was necessary, it was stopped so that she would not shoot past the man in the water, she almost ceased to swing and glided slowly, gradually losing her way. Now was the crucial time, for if another aircraft came in she would find a sitting target. Tommy was aware of the risks he ran in trying to save one man. If he had been one of those ruthless types who are reputed to win wars, and who die unsung, he would have driven on. 'After all,' he might have argued, 'we're all likely to be blotted out in the immediate future, either all together, or one at a time. Bert Toogood may well be glad to have such an easy way out. Drowning is preferable to most ways and practically painless.'

But such a course had no appeal to him. If wars had to be won by such methods then life was not worth living. Tommy was captain, not only of his ship, but of his soul.

He looked through his glasses at the small bobbing head, calculated the distance and nodded to Bert Davis waiting the word to go over the side.

Bert went in with a beautiful swallow dive, towing the line behind him. As soon as he was in the water he struck out vigorously and was soon well on his way to Toogood, who was swimming to meet him. At the same moment an enemy fighter plane came down almost vertically, spraying the submarine with machine-gun bullets. Although not caught completely unawares, and although the small guns were immediately brought to bear, the attack was something in the way of being a surprise. Splinters and bullets flew everywhere. Two more men were hit and this time Tommy got his first scratch. He was holding up his glasses, still watching the rescuer, when a splinter knocked them out of his hands. They spun violently in the air and fell over the side and with them went the tip of the little finger of his right hand.

He stuck it in his mouth and sucked it until a few moments later Morgan Jones arrived with a temporary dressing. In the meantime the swimmers, with what appeared to be agonising sloth, had nearly reached each other. By now Davis' life-line was expended and he was forced to tread water and to wait for Toogood to reach him. Toogood was an indifferent swimmer, and hampered by his clothes. He appeared to be taking it easy, but in fact he was doing his best. In the meantime the *Gauntlet* was forced to lie stopped.

'Aircraft dead astern!'

Round went the guns. It was a biggish bomber, by the look of it, coming in with a deliberation that was portentous. Unless avoiding action was taken this was likely to be the end.

'Megaphone!' Tomy ordered. The trumpet was put into his hands. 'Hang on, both of you!' he yelled. 'I'm going ahead.'

Whether they heard or not it didn't matter, for that moment the two swimmers met and were hauled back to the submarine by the three-inch gun's crew.

'Full ahead, starboard! Hard-a-port!' Tommy ordered.

The engines rumbled into action before the swimmers were inboard; they swung astern on their life-line and luckily were not on the side of the turning propeller. It took the efforts of several men to haul them in and they were considerably bruised by the battering they got alongside the hull. But there was no time for commiseration, or apology; the bomber was close on them. Away streaked the guns' crews and as the enemy got close it received full salvoes from all the guns. Such a determined defence affected the actions of the enemy pilot immediately. He put his machine into a steep climb and dropped his bombs prematurely. Another life had been granted to the *Gauntlet*.

Tommy, almost oblivious of the pain in his finger, looked at his watch disbelievingly. It couldn't be only ten o'clock. Surely his watch had stopped! But it hadn't. Eight hours to darkness – what a hope! Suddenly he felt ravenous. He spied Davis quietly returning to his station and gave him a mild pat on the back. 'Nice work, Davis,' he said. The man grinned.

'That's all right, sir,' he said.

The words didn't mean much but his grin meant everything. His arms and shoulders were livid where he had been pulled along the steel hull, but he too, in company with all the slightly hurt on board, wasn't thinking of his injuries any more than a footballer feels his hacks; after the game was over they might all stiffen up and ache, but not now.

'I'm hungry,' said Tommy.

'O.K., sir,' said the Flunkey.

'What the devil do you want?' asked Tommy plaintively. Izzy Sammons was crawling between his legs to attack the chart table.

'Don't mind me, sir,' said the little Jew, 'just carry on.'

'Oh, it's you Sammons,' said Tommy, 'come for the chart table?'

'That's the idea, sir. No, don't move, I can manage. Besides,' he added with a leer, 'you'll stop anythink comin' my way.'

'Always did 'ave an eye for the main chance,' said Guts. 'Let's 'ave a look at that finger o' yours, sir.'

Tommy took his hand out of his pocket and showed the neatly bandaged stump. 'It's all right thank you, cox'n,' he said. 'Mr Morgan Jones has fixed it for me.'

The coxswain sucked his teeth noisily. 'Oh, 'e 'as,' he said. 'Any other orders, sir?'

'Yes,' said Tommy, 'push round some bully-beef sandwiches and lime juice. We're all pretty peckish up here.'

'Anything you say,' said Guts, adding as a relief to his injured feelings, 'you there, Tucket, go easy with that bucket.'

He couldn't understand why everybody howled with laughter. It wasn't as funny as all that, but everybody must have his safety-valve. If the *Gauntlet* survived this ordeal the saga of Tucket and his bucket would pass into the repertoire of vintage submarine stories, generously endowed, no doubt, with more words of a similar sound.

But only ten o'clock! – a long way to go for a respite!

CHAPTER THIRTEEN

The Gannet, leaning his forehead heavily against the rubber cushion of the layer's telescopic sight, gritted his teeth as another wave of nausea swept through him. It was all right when he was pulling the trigger, or trying to get his sights on an aircraft, but in the intervals he felt as sick as a dog. What with the natural feeling of fear for the outcome of this encounter, and the wretched condition of his inside, he was like the classic example of the sea-sick passenger whose state of mind varied between being afraid he was going to die and the awful fear that he was not.

Anyway he was better off up in the air, taking part in the battle, than lying on a bunk down below, in ignorance of what was going on. If only his belly would stop aching. He kept thinking of the story of the boy with the fox gnawing into his vitals – must have been a brave chap, braver than anyone here. What a jam they were in. He wondered how his parents would take it if he didn't get back. They had been pretty well knocked out when he told them that he had volunteered for submarines. His father, that very English baronet, who specialised in the understatement of facts, had said with one eyebrow lifted: 'Was that really necessary?' and then had joined a bomb-disposal squad. His mother was already working herself to rags in a women's voluntary service. They both felt a great deal about the Baronetcy, and 'passing things on'; the Gannet's sublime disregard for such matters was both a source of disappointment and of admiration to his devoted parents, who prided themselves on their broadmindedness, and made genuine efforts to laugh at their son's eccentricities. Any young man who lacked pride in his family must be a little out of the ordinary, but that showed his sense of individuality, so that was all right. 'Nice people,' thought the Gannet, 'they'll miss me.' And then: 'I wish another aircraft would come and get this over.'

'Like a sandwich, sir?' The Flunkey was standing beside

the gun with a plate of hard biscuit and some slices of bully beef. 'Go on, sir,' he said, 'it'll put some heart into you.' The Gannet shook his head.

'Could you go an egg?' – the Flunkey produced a hard-boiled egg with the polished skill of a conjurer. The Gannet shook his head again.

'Got any water?' he murmured. Out came a water bottle. He took a pull and felt stronger. The Flunkey pressed a bar of chocolate into his hand and passed on to Tommy, whose appetite was unimpaired by the sense of appalling disaster which pressed on all around him. Tommy had long since discovered the art of subduing the imagination. The secret lay in throwing one's whole weight into the problems on hand. If he once allowed the process of thought to stray along the paths of reason, the inevitable destination must become despair. At present he was hungry. So he ate voraciously. When the enemy came again he would fight the action with all his energies. Beyond that there was no point in thinking. Any reasonable person who considered the condition of affairs for those aboard the *Gauntlet* would say that they were done for. The logical follow-up of that statement was, that since they were done for they had better make the best terms for themselves with the enemy. After all why waste valuable lives? How many victories have been handed on a plate to an enemy by such logical reasoning? Long-term planning might be all right at headquarters, but here one had to meet one's problems as each one arose. Tommy looked at his watch again. Eleven o'clock. Seven hours to go. He swallowed the last bit of his hard boiled egg with difficulty and washed it down with a pull from the water bottle. Immediately underneath him, Izzy Sammons with hammer and chisel, was knocking the heads off the rivets which secured the chart table into position. To the right the weary and begrimed face of the top man in the bucket party showed in the open conning-tower hatch. They'd been hoisting buckets for two hours now. If they were getting tired already the prospects were bleak. As he saw it – a hundred hours would be the minimum requirement. A hundred hours – perish the thought!

He went to the voice-pipe and called for Bill. 'Can you afford to give the bucket party a spell – say five minutes in the hour – they may have to go on for a bit yet?' he said.

'I can't really, sir,' said Bill, 'but I see your point. I'll give 'em five minutes in the hour.'

'How's the ammunition supply?' asked Tommy.

'Not too bad at present,' said Bill, 'plenty of Oerlikon left anyhow.'

'How is the gun?'

'Better than it was. Only jams every fifth round or so. How's your finger, sir?'

'I'd forgotten about it,' said Tommy, as indeed he had. 'You may have to relieve the Sub any time now. He's looking a bit green.'

'Shall I come up?' There was eagerness in Bill's voice.

'No. Not till I say. There's one thing you should do though.'

'Yes, sir?'

'Get all the coded messages, and sailing orders, and so forth, and have 'em handy for burning. You never know. Might as well be careful.'

'I see, sir.' There was a little silence as the implications were digested. 'What about the confidential books? Shall I sack them up?'

'Might as well,' Tommy's voice was casual. 'I'll give you a word for it. "Cheese and Biscuits." "Cheese" is to burn all papers. "Biscuits" ditch all C.Bs.'

'Cheese and Biscuits,' repeated Bill. 'What's the weather like up top?'

'In our favour,' lied Tommy. 'Flying must be very tricky. With any luck they might not find us again.'

Whoomph! A high-level bomb burst a few hundred yards away.

'Cancel my last remark,' said Tommy. 'Anyway they're keeping at a respectful distance.'

'Aircraft coming in Green four-oh!' The action blazed up again anew. This time it was a cannon-firing aircraft, fortunately inexpertly flown. They survived the attack with only one casualty.

Down in the torpedo-room Morgan Jones was tasting for the first time the awful experience of running a casualty clearing station. Men were being brought in bleeding profusely and suffering from the first shock of being wounded and finding themselves alive. Blood was everywhere, but Morgan Jones didn't mind that. He had a good stomach. What he hated so much was seeing and hearing good men broken down by pain. Like most Welshmen he had his proper share of imagination; it had been because he was able to visualise scenes such as these that he had run away from hospital to sea. Now fate, with a grim sense of humour, had caught him up. As long as he was sewing up and dressing wounds he was pretty well all right, but when there was nothing of that sort to do he began to hear the things he had so much wished to avoid; and all the time he was being watched by Guts Hinton. Guts was convinced that the young reserve officer would not be able to take it. He hung round helping wherever possible and preparing himself for the moment when he would lead the retching Navigator away from the patients and get on with the job himself. Somehow Morgan Jones knew what was at the back of the coxswain's mind. It made him decide not on any account to let his weakness get the better of him.

The torpedo-room was quiet enough for any hospital. It heaved a bit in the usual swell and it rattled as the vibration of the engine picked up a period. Every now and again a wave could be heard, thundering across the casing, every now and again the coxswain would go aft to the control-room to see how things were faring. In the compartment itself the wounded suffered in various degrees of silence. One, whose pain was greater than his injury, was chain-smoking and swearing under his breath. One was in a sort of delirium and calling again and again for Eileen. Two were right 'out' with morphia and one lay vomiting.

'*Eileen! Eileen! Eileen!*' It was heart-rending.

'Put a sock in it, old man,' called the smoker.

Morgan Jones looked at his diminishing stock of morphia and gave the patient another shot. (*Eileen! Eileen! Eileen!*)

'That's 'is wife,' said the coxswain. 'Just 'ad a nipper, she 'as. You feeling all right, sir?'

'I'm hungry,' said the Navigator. 'Go along and see if you can get me something to eat.' It was a brave thing to say. The coxswain looked disappointed.

'Sure you ought to 'ave anything, sir? You're lookin' a bit peaky to me.'

(*Eileen! Eileen! Eileen!*)

'Will you do as you're told, please.'

The *Gauntlet* rattled and banged as the armament opened fire. The coxswain went away and the Navigator held his aching head. He *would* carry on whatever happened, just to show that pig-faced blighter who thought he hadn't got the nerve.

(*Eileen! Eileen! Eileen!*)

The dope was taking effect. The voice was slurred and much of the poignancy had gone out of it. Soon it dropped to a series of grunts, and for one moment there was complete silence. Then Morgan Jones heard footsteps, and saw his tormentor returning empty-handed. He was shaken by something, that was clear; he slumped down on the door-step and held his head.

'Cor,' he said, 'they're in a proper pot-mess aft in the control-room. Water everywhere and the air's thick with chlorine!'

CHAPTER FOURTEEN

It was Bill Brown who first got the unmistakable whiff of chlorine gas in his nostrils. It was not very strong and he was not surprised. It only needs a few drops of salt water in the sulphuric acid of a battery cell and the current would do the rest. Fortunately it couldn't steal on you like other gasses. You could smell it and you could, if it was concentrated, see it as well. As long as the hatch was open and the engine continued to suck the air down it, there was no real danger. He decided to keep this bit of bad news away from the Skipper and said nothing about it until one of the bucket party began to cough desperately. Then, for the first time, Bill thought he saw a faint gleam of yellowish vapour rising from between the battery boards. Obviously something must be done. He went to the main switchboard and pulled the fuses of number three battery, thus cutting off one third of the vessel's electricity supply. Once the passage of electric current through the affected cells was stopped the generation of gas would practically cease. But what a blow to lose one third of their precious store of electricity! With a heavy heart he climbed past the bucket chain to tell Tommy the latest bit of bad news. It was raining heavily now and the aircraft attacks had momentarily ceased. The visibility was down to about five miles. Tommy's spirits were rising. To have survived three hours of everything the Japanese air force could do was a considerable feat of arms. Now, a great deal depended upon the ability of the Japanese pilots to assess the damage they had done. If they were anything like some of the 'birdmen' Tommy had met they would by now be telling the Intelligence Officer that the submarine was well and truly pranged, and they might be believed. Some of the bomb bursts had completely enshrouded the *Gauntlet* in smoke and spray. It would be justifiable for any airman to assume that he had inflicted mortal damage, but Tommy was afraid that the Japanese air force in the Andaman Islands had been idle for some time, and were likely to be very zealous as long as there was anything of a target showing above water.

Tommy saw the look on Number One's face and whistled slowly as he heard the bad news. 'Never mind,' he said presently – 'we'll deal with it when it gets dark. How's the Chief getting on?'

'He's got his fingers crossed. He's trying to mend the starboard engine but the spare gear is all under water and it's going to be a long job. He'll have the circulating pump working in about half an hour, he says.'

'That's something,' said Tommy and turned afresh to search the horizon with a spare pair of glasses.

'If only this rain keeps on,' he said, 'every hour puts us six miles farther away. When it gets dark we'll make a big alteration of course and hope that they lose us during darkness and don't pick us up again in the morning.'

'D'you hear that?' asked Bill.

They listened. A number of planes were passing directly overhead but were hidden in a rain cloud.

'What a let off,' said Tommy, 'must have been at least half a dozen. Let me know if things get any worse.'

'Aye, aye,' said Bill and went reluctantly below. The air still stank villainously of chlorine but the concentration was harmless. He watched the bucket party for a while and then went in search of reliefs. Now that the guns were not firing the ammunition supply party could give a hand for a while.

On the bridge Tommy saw the visibility close down to half a mile or so, as the rain fell heavily. The curtain was well and truly down; he prayed that it would stay that way until darkness came. Every minute that passed increased their chances of survival, and with this hope came the lifting of his self-imposed ban on thinking outside the immediate present. He wondered for a moment where Audrey was, and what she would say when he told her all about this. With this thought came the first feeling of remorse at having landed himself and the crew in such a predicament. He ought not to have surfaced. He should have been more patient. If he had only waited a little longer! What a tale to have to tell on paper when he returned to harbour with an unserviceable submarine, and half his crew as casualties. The casualties were something he'd never experienced before. That was usually one blessing of the submarine life, that the war was carried on in an abstract manner. One fired a torpedo, or a gun, at a distant enemy and never saw the pain and destruction caused by one's own weapons. The enemy's retaliation took the form of depth charges and bombs. They either missed you, or blotted you out; there was no half-way business of men ripped to pieces by splinters and dying in agony. Death – . That reminded him that he would have to bury the dead at sea. He'd never done that before. He'd read about it and it had always seemed to be terribly dramatic. 'We now commit his body to the deep.' Distressing business.

The rain sizzled down, flattening the sea with its sheer weight.

Izzy Sammons crawled out from under the bridge canopy and grinned affably at his Captain. 'We'll soon 'av a proper patch on 'er,' he said. He was positively cheerful. 'Excoosey mar,' he said as he squeezed past the bucket chain. 'Je churchai le strong-back.'

'Wot's up with you, Chiefy,' barracked a seaman.

'It's the French blood in me,' said Izzy. He dropped out of sight and the weary clank of buckets was resumed.

Tommy was not a particularly religious man, but he was a practising Christian; that is to say, he went to church on Sundays, if there was nothing better to do, and he got up early on feast days. It was some time since he'd knelt down to say his prayers in formal fashion. He wished now that he hadn't given it up. He couldn't very well say a prayer now, just because he was in a jam. He had a feeling that God (if there was God – he wasn't absolutely sure about that) would laugh like a drain to see the gallant Tommy Woodstock crying out for help. 'The devil was sick, the devil a monk would be.' All the same he owed it to his ship's company to try anything and everything. Not for himself but for the wounded and dying.

He half closed his eyes and said a prayer. 'These chaps don't deserve to die,' he said, 'they are absolutely tip-top and full of guts. Just because I made a mistake it's not fair to take it out on them. Just keep this rain going, please God, until dark and I'll manage the rest somehow.' Then he said the Lord's Prayer just to add good measure, and that was that. He felt like someone who had just posted a most important letter. Now he must wait and see whether the 'usual channels' would yield a favourable answer.

It didn't take long to see that his request had misfired. Within five minutes the rain began to ease off – the visibilty was improving rapidly. He looked at his watch. It had been thick for over an hour. Whilst the curtain was down many things could have been happening behind it.

'Tell the First-Lieutenant to close up all supply parties,' he said down the voice-pipe, 'the visibility is getting better.' He turned to the guns' crews. 'Stand by, everybody!' he said. The rain cloud was moving rapidly away, impelled by a fresh and cooling breeze. Out to windward there was no sign of enemy activity, but what lay in store for them to leeward? They'd soon know now. He dried off the eye-piece of his binoculars and stood waiting. Serve him bloody well right for having the cheek to ask for God's assistance. Must be half-daft.

He searched the receding horizon, hoping against hope to see nothing. Steadily he trained his glasses a few degrees at a time. Half the horizon to leeward was clear but – what was that? His heart began to thump as he saw what all along he had feared he would see, the long grey outline of an enemy warship, not more than six miles away and steering parallel to *Gauntlet*'s course. He went to the voice-pipe and asked for the First-Lieutenant.

Any minute now the enemy would open fire.

'Sir?' came Bill's cheerful voice.

'Enemy frigate in sight!' said Tommy. 'Cheese and Biscuits!'

CHAPTER FIFTEEN

THIS then must be the end. The frigate had only to turn towards the *Gauntlet* and open fire, and the day would be hers. She would probably be armed with three or four biggish guns. The only thing for *Gauntlet* to do was to try and torpedo her and, if that failed, to ram her. Desperate measures indeed. 'Get all torpedoes ready,' ordered Tommy.

'Six aircraft!' reported the signalman.

They came roaring down out of the clouds, each one dropping a stick of bombs. For the next few minutes the sea round *Gauntlet* was a mass of white pinnacles of water, much of which actually fell on them, but not a bomb hit them. To the watching frigate it must appear to be certain destruction; perhaps that was why she had not so far opened fire. Almost before the last cascade of foaming water had subsided, came another six bombers. Once again the stuff fell round them, exploding as it reached the water, and once again the *Gauntlet* emerged unscathed. Tommy kept her swinging madly about by means of full rudder, and, as a form of deception, he caused her to be listed over so that a distant watcher might think she was mortally hit. Away to windward another patch of heavy rain was in sight. 'If,' argued Tommy, 'the Japanese air force are as cagey about targets as some of the ones I know in the RAF, they may have told the Navy to leave us alone. Some big pot working up for the Order of the Crimson Carnation or some such!' He looked long and carefully at the frigate. Her guns were not even trained. Incredible though it might seem it was perfectly clear that the frigate was only watching. The rain cloud was getting nearer.

Three fighter planes came out of nowhere and raked the bridge with machine-gun fire. Two men were hit and no damage was inflicted upon the enemy. These vicious gun attacks were impossible to avoid. Each one would bring fresh casualties. While the unfortunate wounded were bundled below another high-level attack raised more plumes of water. And then, as a blessed relief, the curtain dropped again, and heavy rain blotted everything out. Tommy steadied the *Gauntlet* on to her course, and was amazed to be alive. At that moment Bill Brown's head appeared in the hatch-way.

'I've done the deed, sir,' he said, 'here are the biscuits.'

'Pack 'em on the after part of the bridge,' said Tommy, 'but don't ditch them until I say. Don't look now,' he said, 'but it's come down thick again.'

Overhead they could hear the droning of many planes, like a swarm of angry gnats. Once a bomb fell remarkably close, though whether it was dropped by accident or design they would never know.

This time the rain seemed to have come to stay. Tommy watched a whole hour go past and sent a postcard to God apologising for his apparent lack of faith. Once again his spirits began to rise. They had come through so far, might it not be possible to come through to the end?

''Arf a minute, 'Swain,' came a plaintive voice as Guts Hinton forced himself up to the open hatch-way. 'Permission to serve out rum, sir?' he asked.

Tommy wondered for a while whether it was wise at this juncture to allow it.

'It'll put 'eart into 'em, sir,' said Guts.

'Um,' said Tommy. 'I'm not sure that they need that.'

'It's for you to say, sir,' said Guts.

'I know it is,' said Tommy. Then he made up his mind. 'All right.' he said, 'but regulation tots only, and tell the First-Lieutenant to supervise the issue.'

The coxswain gave his Captain a reproachful look for not trusting him, and his full-moon face vanished below.

The rain continued to pour down.

Tommy began to think of ways and means.

Down in the torpedo-room Morgan Jones swallowed his tot and felt a little better. In the engine-room the water surged and swished over the footways, but it had not risen for over an hour. Mr Miles's efforts with the circulating pump were bearing fruit. For the first time since the hull was breached they were holding their own. But there were still four hours of daylight and safety lay seven hundred miles away.

Then time began to take a hand. The seconds which had lumbered painfully past once more ticked merrily into minutes and hours. After the stress and strain of the first part of the day a sort of sizzling somnolence prevailed over the upper part of the submarine. The men at the guns drooped with a strange weariness, born of emotions not often experienced; for they had faced the inevitable bravely and were still, unaccountably, alive.

Tommy found it increasingly difficult to remain alert. The rain hissed and poured, the sea was flattened down as if the heavy roller had been used. The sound of aircraft droning futilely overhead was practically continuous, and somewhere not far distant, no doubt, a warship was groping her way in search of her prey. It wasn't a nice position, but Tommy had frequently to tell himself to keep on his toes (as the Staff-Officer would have put it).

Every now and again, however, the curtain of rain would partly rise and glimpses of a horizon some two or three miles distant were vouchsafed. Then Tommy would feverishly search for signs of surface vessels and then he would begin to see them. Before his ardent gaze figments would steam into view, flotillas of destroyers, cruisers, every manner of ship would appear like ghosts, only to fade into nothing on closer inspection. More than once Tommy was within an ace of ditching the signal books. The whole sea seemed to be populated with these ghost ships. Then the rain would thicken and blot out his hallucinations.

And the minutes went by. Down in the after part of the control-room Izzy Sammons, with the aid of an electric drill, was boring a second hole in the vicinity of the breached hull. When it was complete bolts would be inserted so that the covering patch which he had beaten into shape could be hove down over the damaged part. Four thicknesses of blanket, coated with a mixture known as Medley's Compound, were to form the soft seating of the patch, which would be practically water-tight. Meanwhile the combined efforts of the bucket chain and the pump were beginning to show results. The level in the engine-room was two inches down and the *Gauntlet* was riding easier on the surface. This extraordinary respite from enemy attack was at first so miraculous that everybody's spirits were raised. Now, the absence of the enemy was taken for granted and as people had time to observe the true situation a deep and desperate gloom settled upon them. Only Tommy, who had not so far left the bridge since he had surfaced the *Gauntlet*, was immune from this feeling of deep despair. He alone had not seen the appalling state of things in the submarine, he had not seen the torpedo-room, as full of wounded men as any cockpit of Nelson's time, but he could sense the feeling of 'let-down' and knew now that in order to save his ship he would have to get tough with his crew. When darkness came they would want to relax. Only strength of will on the part of the officers would keep them going.

Presently the Flunkey came up with a mug of tea. To his surprise Tommy's watch showed four o'clock. It would be dark in about two hours. As he lifted the steaming cup to his lips Tommy became aware that the rain was ceasing. Away up to windward it was getting lighter. As he watched he saw the visibility growing before his eyes; veil after veil of mist was lifted as if in some grand pantomine transformation scene. What would be revealed when the last viel had gone?

He went to the voice-pipe and warned everybody. Then he waited the completion of the transformation scene.

Now visibility to windward was maximum, and, still there was nothing in sight. So far so good, but what about the lee side? And where were the enemy aircraft?

For the first time since the beginning of it all Tommy's knees felt wobbly; the strain of waiting to see was almost unbearable.

'Get up on the periscope standard,' he said to the signalman, 'and see if you can see anything.' The man clambered up, and with practised eye swept the whole horizon.

'What can you see?'

'Nothin' as yet,' said the signalman, and then qualified the statement. 'Arf a mo, sir.'

He levelled his glass for some time and then summed up the situation.

'Small patch o' smoke and a top mast,' he said. 'I reckon it's every bit of eight miles away.'

'Which way is she going?'

'Couldn't say, sir.'

'Stay up there and watch her.'

'Aircraft!'

A lone bomber was flying high overhead. They watched and waited but no attack took place. Away on the port horizon several more machines were circling and diving upon some unrevealing target which they were far too busy attacking to look elsewhere. At that moment the port engine exhaust began to pour out black smoke. Tommy felt like screaming abuse down the voice-pipe at Mr Miles, but managed to temper his exasperation.

'Tell the Chief that if he can't stop making smoke he must stop the engine,' he said mildly enough.

There was a distant 'Aye! aye!' and a minute later the recalcitrant Diesel valve was cut out. As the light slowly failed they tiptoed away from the scene, unable to believe their good fortune. Then, as the visibility was such that an appeal against the light would have been sustained by any umpire, a bomber, accompanied by two fighter bombers, suddenly appeared. They circled round the luckless submarine, weaving patterns in and out of the clouds so that it was impossible to keep the guns on the target. Then, suddenly, the two smaller planes came down with everything blazing. Their object clearly was to demoralise the defence in preparation for the bomber to come in and finish the job. Their shooting was erratic but their aerobatics were superb. They dived and swooped, rolled and banked, distributing their favours over a wide area. Small bombs, cannon shell and machine-gun bullets were whizzing in all directions. Finally, by some prearranged signal, they hauled off and the big bomber came roaring in. *Gauntlet,* with full rudder on, swerved violently, all her guns were trained upon the attacker but he came in until they could see the little men aboard her and then the men at the guns saw two heavy bombs leaving their stowage. Down they came together, falling close under the *Gauntlet*'s port quarter where they exploded under water with tremendous force. The submarine was picked up and shaken by the explosions, and those below waited for the sound of rushing water. But the vessel's hull was stoutly constructed and apart from starting some minor leaks she was apparently unharmed.

Away flew the bomber and back came the lighter craft, but by now it was too dark for safe flying and they soon withdrew.

Tommy watched them go with little sense of relief. Now that they knew that *Gauntlet* was still afloat, the Japanese would lay on an even more efficient attack in the morning. If only the rain could have lasted until dark. He took himself in hand and thought of the little old nursemaid who had taught him to sing 'Count your blessings one by one.'

They had survived. Tomorrow was another day.

He imagined what the Staff-Officer would have said about this affair. 'The first part of the planned withdrawal must consist of making every attempt to disengage from the enemy. After that the defences could be strengthened and preparations made for the possible resumption of hostilities on the ensuing day.' Just so!

He heard a voice at his ear. 'Shall we fall out the guns' crews now, sir?' It was Bill Brown still as calm and collected as he had been at the beginning of it all. Tommy banished his fears for tomorrow.

'Yes, please,' he said. 'Get me out a list of defects. I'll come down and have a look at things shortly.'

It was strangely quiet now on the bridge. The smell of cordite smoke still lingered in his nostrils but the men had gone. Once again the *Gauntlet* took on that extraordinary purposeful rhythm as she breasted the little waves. The night was soft and dark. Thank God there was no moon. Thank God those last bombs had missed. Thank God for chaps like Bill Brown. Thank God –

CHAPTER SIXTEEN

As soon as Morgan Jones was available to take his trick on the bridge, Tommy left him there sucking in great gulps of air, uncontaminated by the smells of suffering humanity, and went below for a tour of inspection with his First-Lieutenant.

It was much worse than anything he had imagined. Coming upon a state of chaos, which by now had been accepted by everyone else, was a great shock. Tommy was seeing the damage *in toto*, whereas the crew had become accustomed to it a piece at a time, and were carrying on in their bizarre surroundings as if it was the most natural thing in the world to walk up to one's knees in water, through a chlorine-ridden atmosphere, in almost total darkness. As he reached the bottom of the control-room ladder, a man walked past him carrying two cups of tea and shouting: 'Char's up, come and get it.' The men on the bucket chain suspended operations and shuffled forward for refreshment. Tommy looked round him. Was this the trim and shining control-room that he had left but ten short hours ago? Were the haggard and filthy men he saw around him his crew? While he had been lording it on the bridge, fighting back with proper weapons against the forces of nature that gave no quarter and did not draw stumps at close of play. He suddenly felt a tremendous surge of pride that in all this misfortune not one little wail of despair had reached his ears. What a good thing it had been that he, up top, had not been able to visualise the state of affairs below.

'H'm,' he said, as he took in the details of the damage, 'bit of a mess, isn't it?' He walked over and examined the hole in the hull, through which protruded the dripping blanket-plug which Toogood had inserted, how many years ago? He must see that the man was given the highest recognition for this act, funny to think that it was only a few days back that Toogood had tried to get out of it all.

'How's the patch getting on?' he asked.

'I've got it here, sir,' said Izzy, producing his masterpiece with great pride.

'Is it ready?' asked the Captain.

'As soon as I got me strong-backs in place, sir.'

'Can you fit it in the dark?'

'Doubtful, sir.'

Tommy looked troubled. 'Bit risky showing a light up there,' he said and left the decision open. A great deal would depend upon the weather. He waded into the engine-room, trying to show the same disregard for the appalling conditions as the rest of the party. Mr Miles greeted him with the first two parts of a salute. For two pins he would have given the traditional 'all correct, sir.' Tommy looked round the place, at the heaving oil-covered water which splashed him from head to foot, and had enough engineering knowledge to see that it was nothing short of a miracle that the one engine had continued to work. Water must have found its way where water should not be. There seemed to be no reason why the engine should continue to work. The Chief was of the same opinion but said nothing. He, too, was content to live from minute to minute.

Tommy passed on through the deserted motor-room and switch-board to the after compartment where two men wrestled with the hand steering-wheel as if they were undergoing punishment in some private inferno. They brightened a bit at the sight of Tommy and the First-Lieutenant; it gave them a sense of normality. Captain's rounds. If *he* could come off the bridge and wander round the ship – then things couldn't be so bad. Tommy made a futile joke and went back through the control-room and living spaces, to the torpedo-room, and there he felt the full impact of the day's engagement. There were now twelve wounded men and two dead ones in various positions of repose. The atmosphere reeked of disinfectant and vomit. It was nearly dark, for all but one light in the compartment had been switched off. Guts Hinton, fat and happy now that Morgan Jones had gone back to his normal occupation, showed his Captain his charges with a certain pride.

'All doin' as well as can be expected,' he said in a loud voice.

Several of the less dangerously wounded turned to see their Captain. 'Sometime,' thought Tommy, 'I'll go and talk to these men, one at a time; but not now, not now.' He turned and went back to the wardroom where he sat in silence trying to pull himself together. It had been a big dose to take in one spoonful.

Bill Brown watched his Captain and felt reassurance when Tommy pushed his cap to the back of his head and caught the lobe of an ear with the fingers of his right hand, gently massaging it. It was a typical gesture and again suggested a state of normality. Bill slid a sheet of paper under his Captain's eye. Tommy continued to massage his ear, deep in thought.

Bill coughed. 'Here's a list of defects, pretty long I'm afraid,' he said.

'Um?' Tommy came out of his brown study, gave a deep sigh, picked up the paper and read it in detail. It was a frightening document; one engine out of action, pumps out of action, main motors out of action, gyro-compass broken down, wireless-room flooded, steering motors broken, and so on, and so on.

Then the casualty list. Two dead men so far. Tommy lifted his eyes from the paper. 'We'll have to bury them tonight,' he said. 'You're quite certain they are – dead?'

'No doubt at all,' said Bill.

'Make 'em up in a couple of blankets – you'll have to put something at their feet – ' Tommy's voice trailed off. 'The sooner the better,' he went on – speaking from a great distance – 'bad for morale to keep 'em lying about – can't wait till daylight. How's the ammunition supply?'

'Enough for a couple of attacks.'

'That's all?'

'I'm afraid so.'

'How are the batteries?'

'Getting a bit low but they should last another forty-eight hours.'

'No chance of charging them?'

'Not a hope.'

Tommy started to doodle as he absorbed the details of the situation. Presently he spoke:

'Forty-eight hours won't be enough,' he said, 'nothing like. We shouldn't get more than half-way.' He went on with rather an impressive doodle, and saw into the possible future. A submarine, slowly filling up with water, a quarter of her crew incapacitated, her engines stopped for lack of electric power, total darkness below, feverish attempts to build rafts from anything that floated – sharks – the inevitable plunge, which would finish the tragedy. Alternatively, a direct hit when the attacks were resumed at daylight. Quicker and more certain. He finished the doodle and looked at his second-in-command. Bill's attitude was grave and pre-occupied, but there was no indication in his manner of despair.

'I suppose,' he said, 'there's no other submarine in these parts?'

'I doubt it,' said Tommy. '*Goose* was due to go on patrol, but her engines were out of order when we left. Anyway, we don't know where she would be even if she has gone. Let's have a talk with Toogood. I want to know about the wireless. If we could repair it our troubles would be nearly all over.'

'Pass the word for the P.O. Tel.,' called Bill.

Bert Toogood limped in. His feet were very painful and he ached all over from his battering against the submarine's hull.

'Sit down,' said Tommy.

Bert sat.

'If we get the wireless cabinet pumped out, could you transmit?' asked Tommy.

'No, sir,' said Bert.

'Why not?'

'All our generators are wet to start with and the condensers and the potentiometers – and – '

Tommy interrupted him. 'Quite out of the question?'

'Quite.'

'That's that.'

'Of course,' said Toogood, 'I could rig up a simple receiver set.'

'That's not much good,' said Bill.

'Half a minute,' said Tommy, 'it's better than nothing.'

'I don't see,' said Bill.

'If we intercepted a signal from a boat on patrol we might know where she was.'

'But there aren't any on patrol within five hundred miles,' said Bill.

'Not as far as we know,' said Tommy, 'but there's always a chance that *Goose* might be sent this way.'

'*Goose*!' Bert Toogood practically exploded with excitement as he said it.

'What is it, Toogood?' asked Tommy.

'I just remembered, sir. A signal from *Carpentaria*, just as the shot hit us.'

'What did it say?'

'It said when she was sailing, her position, course and speed and her patrol position. But I can't remember the details.'

Tommy looked at Bill. 'When you burnt the papers I told you about, did you look at them to see what they were?'

Bill shook his head. 'I'm afraid not, sir. I was in a hurry and my hand was shaking like a jelly.'

'What did you do with the signal?' asked Tommy.

Bert thought for a moment. 'I decyphered it and copied it into the log.'

'Then it's in the cabinet now?'

'Yes, sir. Shall I get it?'

'Yes, please. You'll have to put on an escape apparatus and get in there somehow. Be as quick as you can. It's vital.'

'Aye, aye, sir.'

Tommy blew out his cheeks with relief. Here was hope indeed. If *Goose* was anywhere within a distance of two hundred miles or so, they might make contact with her. It wasn't much to build hopes on but it was something and by heaven! they needed something.

He began another doodle. Supposing that it was possible to make contact with a friend before the electricity supply ran out what was the next most important thing in the problem? In answer to his question came the sound of a clattering bucket and a string of obscenity from some weary member of the chain who had stopped it with his head. Forty-eight hours more bailing and they'd all be mad. He looked at the expectant Bill.

'We'd better get that patch on while the weather holds,' he said. 'I don't like having a light on deck but it's the choice of evils. Tell Sammons to go right ahead. Take a deck-cloth up and try to shroud the light.'

'Ay, aye, sir.'

'Better attend to it yourself.'

'I was going to.'

'Come back when you've done it.'

Bill went out and Tommy went on with his thoughts, pursuing them to the end. It would be a pity if they didn't win through. What was it that Scott had written?

'Had we lived I should have had a tale to tell of the hardihood, courage, and endurance of my companions which would have stirred the heart of every Englishman.'

Curious trait of the English; they invariably got themselves into a proper mess, due to insufficient preparation, or foolhardy courage, and then performed prodigies of valour in extracting themselves from positions they should never have got into. A deep sigh interrupted his meditations and he became aware for the first time that the Gannet was fast asleep in his bunk. Tommy stood up, walked to the bed side. The Gannet looked about fourteen in his sleep. His breathing was regular and his cheeks were no longer flushed. It looked as if the original problem which had started this unhappy train of events was about to solve itself. The Gannet was recovering just in time to take the rap with the rest of them. Where had it all gone wrong? Why had he not waited before surfacing to engage the enemy? All this could have been saved by a more skilful commanding officer. Now he was responsible already for the deaths of two of his men and he didn't rate the others' chances very high. It was that incurable defect in his make-up. A tendency to let up at the wrong moment. He was born lazy, that was it. Why, what was he doing down here when there was important work on deck?

He got up and went on to the bridge squeezing his way past a profane and weary bucket chain.

'If that patch works,' he said cheerfully, 'you won't have to do that much longer.'

His words gave them fresh heart, and they began to banter as he left them.

''Ere, Tucket,' said one, 'go easy with that bucket.'

'What's up wi' you, Charlie; ain't you 'appy in your work?'

'This is the one thousandth seven hundred and forty bleedin'-second blinking bucket I've emptied, Mr Tucket.'

''Course I've counted 'em that's why.'

''Ear what the Skipper said?'

''Ow far we from 'ome?'

''Couple a fousand miles, I shouldn't wonder.'

'Cor, what a turn up for the book.'

''Ere, Lofty, what about a cup o' char?'

'Bucket comin' up!'

It was very dark and the air was sweet. Bill Brown was leaning over the after end directing the rays of a pocket-torch on Izzy Sammons who was down on the casing with his patch. Though it was as calm as those conditions of weather would ever permit, a good deal of water kept washing over the hull, making work there a difficult and hazardous task. Izzy Sammons got to his feet and spoke.

'Tell you what, sir,' he said, 'if you want to make a job of this you'll 'ave to stop the engine and list 'er well over. Otherwise when I pull out that blanket you'll get a lot of water below.'

He was quite right and Tommy saw it at once, but he didn't relish the idea of lying stopped on the surface, and showing a light on deck, one little bit. Four years of war had made him allergic to loitering on the surface and it took a great effort of will to postpone a decision, or to put off the evil hour until they had put another twenty miles between themselves and the last signs of a surface enemy.

'All right,' he said shortly. 'Tell the engineer officer to speak to me.' (This down the voice-pipe).

'Chief here, sir,' Mr Miles' voice sounded strained.

'Oh Chief,' said Tommy, 'if I stop the engine will it start again?'

There was a pause. 'I don't see why not, sir.'

'No danger – ' persisted Tommy, ' – of water getting somewhere where it shouldn't?'

'I'd rather she went on running,' said Mr Miles, 'but if you must stop her you must.'

'All right,' said Tommy, 'obey the telegraph.'

He waited for Mr Miles to have time to splash his way back to the controls and then wound the handle to 'stop'. The engine rumbled into silence which was relieved by the sound of the opening of the port main-ballast vents. Bill Brown was listing the submarine. The sudden cessation of vibration, coupled with the feeling that the vessel was falling over, brought the coxswain aft at the run. When he heard what was going on he looked reproachfully at Bill Brown. 'You might 'ave given me warnin',' he said, 'I got the wounded to consider.' Then he tramped back to the torpedo-room announcing that: 'Izzy doesn't want to get 'is tootsies wet, so the kind-'earted Jimmy-the-One is obligin' by 'eelin' the sub over.'

Meanwhile Bert Toogood, stark naked, and wearing an

escape apparatus, was groping round the flooded wireless room in pitch darkness, trying to lay his hands on the signal log, or alternatively the sharp pointed file where he stacked his coded signals. The wireless room wasn't much bigger than a telephone box, and yet he had managed to lose his bearings. The trouble was that he kept touching parts of the office which were 'alive', the whole of his body was tingling as if he was in a bed of stinging nettles. It was most disconcerting, and the oxygen which he was breathing made him very stupid. Impossible to think clearly.

He found the little desk with his hands, and pulled his buoyant body down until he should have found the bench on which he had sat for many hundreds of hours. But it wasn't there; being buoyant it had floated to the 'ceiling' of the room. The signal log had been on that bench, goodness knew where it had got to. Out went his hands, feeling along the desk for the pointed file. It wasn't there. Must be somewhere! He pulled himself down into a squatting position and immediately found the file by sitting on its up-turned point. Gingerly he felt down and grasped the thing with its sodden papers and hauled himself up to the open air, where he handed it to his mate with strict injunctions not to disturb it until he came. Then, arming himself with a water-tight torch, he went back into the cabinet to find the log. It took twenty minutes to locate the thing, which was squeezed against the ceiling of the office by the floating bench lockers, and when he was once more in the open air he saw that the log was likely to be of little value, for he had written in it in indelible pencil which, contrary to its name, had dissolved in water, leaving only a purple mess and a few legible words. With feverish haste Toogood found the signal file and extracted the last signal from it. It was nearly pulp but the numbers in the cypher groups were mostly legible. With the aid of a light from the pocket torch he copied the groups afresh on to a dry piece of paper and then went on deck to recover the code books. After half an hour he had succeeded in getting about eighty per cent of the entire message but some of the groups were incorrect and it required a process of elimination to find out which numbers were wrong.

Fortunately for Tommy's peace of mind all this was withheld from him while he watched the work on deck.

As Mr Miles had said, Izzy Sammons was a handy man, and he had the wit and resource of his race which gave him powers of imagination beyond the average. The design and execution of his patch was a piece of brilliant improvisation. It went into position almost without alteration and as he hove down on the bolts securing it the padding squeezed out in a most satisfactory manner.

'If that lot leaks,' said Izzy, 'I'll join the Swiss Navy.'

'Well done, Sammons,' said Tommy, and went to the engine-room telegraph, putting it to 'Half-speed'. Thirty seconds later there was no answering shudder from the engine. Two minutes went to three. Tommy gritted his teeth – the Chief was doing his best. If he couldn't start the damned engine, nobody could.

Meanwhile Bill Brown was blowing the ballast tanks and bringing the *Gauntlet* upright. She now had a watertight hull, but what good would that be if the engine didn't work? Slowly the submarine came up to a vertical position. Izzy watched his patch as the waves once again washed over it and declared it to be a good job. The bucket chain were told that soon as they had got the water out of the ship they wouldn't have to do any more. All was as well as it could be, except for the engine.

'Captain, sir.' Mr Miles only spoke when he had something to say.

'Captain, sir?'

'Yes, Chief.'

'Water in the fuel system – have to strip it all down – couple of hours.'

'Damn,' said Tommy. 'All right, Chief, drive on for all you're worth.'

This was a bitter pill. Everything now depended on that engine, for Mr Miles's verdict on the other one had been most discouraging. Given normal conditions it would have been possible to get it going again, in four hours, or so, but, with things as they were, it would be a very much longer job, and it couldn't be carried out with the other engine running. Nevertheless, thought Tommy, there *are* two engines there and one of them is bloody well *going* to work.

He went below, leaving Morgan Jones on the bridge.

'If you sight anything,' he said, 'press the hooter twice. I'll warn the crew that that means action stations. Gangway!'

Down the ladder he went, squeezing past the buckets into the acrid-smelling control-room and forward to the wardroom where Toogood pored over his books and muttered to himself.

'Any luck?' asked Tommy.

Toogood thrust the signal pad towards him. Tommy read as follows:

'*Carpentaria* to General (and etc.) *Goose* will sail for patrol at nineteen hundred on (blank) passing through position eight degrees north eighty-four degrees east at midnight on (blank) and subsequently patrolling on a north easterly course.' Then followed some details of no importance to this narrative.

'Why the blanks?' asked Tommy. Toogood explained that, by the process of elimination, he had succeeded to the best of his knowledge in getting out the whole message, with the exception of those two groups, which absolutely defied all attempts at intelligent improvisation. It was infuriating. There, on paper, was safety without a doubt, but for two words.

'Nothing more you can do?' he asked.

Toogood was nearly asleep. 'I tried everything, sir,' he said, 'I'm very sorry, sir.'

'Well,' said Tommy, 'all is not lost. If we can get the engine to go and get that position at midnight on the right day, Bob's your uncle. All right, Toogood, you've had a long day. Get a couple of hours' sleep and try again. When you're fresher you may think of something.'

Bert got to his feet and stumbled away, walking like a somnambulist. Tommy stifled a yawn and looked at Bill.

'Tricky,' he said.

Bill nodded. 'Very,' he said and changed the subject. 'Do you feel strong enough to read the burial service, sir?' he inquired, 'we really ought to do it. They're both ready.'

'All right,' said Tommy. 'Bring them into the control-room. I'll read a bit out of the book and then you'll have to hoist 'em up the hatch and ditch them.' He spoke in this manner because it was the safest way to do so. The men who had died were old friends. It didn't seem much of an end to be chucked overboard like a bucket of gash, but what else could they do? He opened his little desk, and took out a prayer book.

The control-room was completely silent as he entered it, except for the sound of hammering which came faintly from the engine-room. The bucket party were standing in a group that any sculptor would have given his back-teeth to see. Naked to their waists, shining with oil and sweat, hair lying damply on foreheads, eyes agleam with fatigue, cheek bones reflecting the high lights in that shadowy compartment, they stood to attention as the bodies swathed and trussed in blankets were laid down on the floor.

'All ready, sir,' said Bill.

Tommy got out his prayer book and read the burial service. He had a sure and certain instinct, had Tommy, that if he showed any perfunctory spirit in the performance of the last rites his men would not forgive him. The simple sailor possesses a very strong sense of rectitude. Tommy went through it all, sought for and found the appropriate words for the committing of the body to the deep and as he read his voice sounded strangely musical.

'We therefore commit his body to the deep to be turned into corruption, looking for the resurrection of the body (when the sea shall give up her dead) and the life of the world to come – '

'Amen.'

'Carry on,' said Tommy.

It took four men to get the awkward bundles on deck. There was a pause and then two dull thuds, as the bodies hit the saddle tanks. 'If I'd thought of it,' said Tommy, 'I'd have listed her over so that they didn't touch. Sorry about that.'

The men accepted his apology. They too had hated the sound of those two dull thuds. Tommy put his cap on and went down into the engine-room. It was no good asking the Chief how he was getting on, but he would very much like to know. Perhaps if he stood and watched he might see for himself.

'Half an hour, sir,' said Mr Miles and bent anew over his work.

Tommy went back to the wardroom and sat down for the first time for fourteen hours.

He had had no intention of sleeping and indeed there was much to be done in preparation for the morning, but within a few minutes of resting his head he went out completely. Bill, who had much to discuss with him, looked at him without resentment but tactfully pulled the wardroom curtain. There would be little sleep for anyone else tonight; it was better not to advertise the Captain's forty winks.

Down in the engine-room the tired fitters were painstakingly stripping and blowing through the entire fuel system. It was a job which could not be hurried, for a single omission might mean a complete repetition of the whole business. Up on the bridge Morgan Jones looked out into the darkness and wondered what the morrow would bring. In his bunk in the wardroom the Gannet was gathering strength in the first pain-free sleep he'd enjoyed for days.

Away up forward Guts tended his wounded with rough and ready sympathy. A drink of water, a smoke, or a shot of pain-killer, were his only means of comforting the sufferers. He went round every half-hour and spent the rest of the time dozing on his capacious haunches, while the *Gauntlet* rocked quietly in the eternal swell.

The bucket-chain was still at it. Bill estimated that another two hours would see them through. He worked them mercilessly, half an hour at a time and then replaced them by others. At the same time a hand-operated pump came into play as the water receded and already the level of all free water was substantially reduced.

When at last the port engine had been completely freed of water, and the source of the trouble removed, Mr Miles blew the engine round by compressed air and reported 'ready' to the bridge. Morgan Jones put the telegraph to ahead. The engine gave a rumble and a reluctant hiss and then burst into a full clattering roar which brought the sleeping Tommy to his feet as if someone had stuck a pin into him. He went stiffly into the control-room, noted the time and stopped to consider the best course to steer. First he plotted *Goose*'s position, then his own, then he joined the two and noted that this course would take him no farther away from the enemy air-fields than he was at present. He debated whether to run out into the 'blue' for twelve hours and then to inch round to his objective during the ensuing night. If he did that, and the engine broke down again, he might not get to the rendezvous by *any* midnight. Of course, if he had known for certain *which* midnight *Goose* would arrive it would have been easier to come to a decision. On the whole, he decided that it was best to crack on for the rendezvous, regardless of the possible consequences. After all, he argued, when an aeroplane can fly at four miles a minute what's a hundred miles or so? Deep down in his mind also was the conviction that two hours more play would finish this particular Test match; but, in case it didn't there was another and very important problem to be solved. What was the error of the magnetic compass, stuck aft in a position in which it was never intended to be used? This must be established immediately but it could only be found if the sky cleared. He went on the bridge. . . . It was still dark and overcast. Nothing to do but wait and hope.

'All right, Pilot,' he said, 'I'll look out now.'

Morgan Jones waited for a moment before saying a reluctant farewell to the softness of that very dark night. Down below his private hell awaited him. He must go to the wounded. He went down and padded softly along to the torpedo-room. It was nearly pitch dark there and almost completely silent. Guts Hinton was asleep, his chin forward, his great mouth sagging wide open, snoring with a harsh repellent rhythm. On one of the bunks a man tossed in pain, swearing softly to himself. Morgan Jones went to him, gave him a drink and settled the blanket roll which served as a pillow. Quietly and methodically he tiptoed round the room and was gratified to find that the great majority of the men were asleep. He went back to the wardroom. Bill Brown had just laid off the bucket chain who stumbled forward, or lay down where they were, to get some rest. They were strong men but the tiredness in that ship was not entirely of the physical variety, it was the fatigue born of overstressed nerves. This constant escape from certain death, the confronting of reason by the unreasonable, was stupefying. They all ought to have been dead long ago, they knew that. For the moment they were too tired to care about the morrow. Bill carefully avoided getting into too comfortable a posture; if he really lay down, he thought, he would pass out completely. So he sat in the Captain's armchair and passed out just the same. Morgan Jones envied him but could not sleep. He lay on his bunk thinking of the treatment which he had given the wounded, reliving every act of surgery and bandaging, recapitulating the diagnoses with an innane sense of glory which overwhelmed him with surprise. Here he was, a man who had bolted from the thought of tending the sick, weary and pain-ridden to the society of the fittest men in the world, only to find that unconsciously he had missed the vocation for which he was undoubtedly suited. As he lay there, breathing the foul air, and sweating into the blankets, he took a vow. If he survived this trip he would go back to the hospital. Of course, people would say that he had cold feet and couldn't face such another ordeal. Let them say!

Over his head the Gannet's bunk creaked as he sat up in it. Morgan Jones looked out and upwards and caught the Gannet's eye.

'How are you?' he whispered.

The Gannet smiled. 'Better,' he said. 'I'll go and give the Skipper a spell.'

He got out of his bunk and Morgan Jones could tell by his movements that he was better. 'An interesting method of treating an inflamed appendix,' he thought.

'I must write to the *Lancet* about it.' He saw the Gannet go aft and then fell asleep.

On the bridge Tommy was watching a little patch in the sky in which there danced a few dimly twinkling stars. If it would only clear to the northerly horizon he could get a bearing of the Pole star. The Gannet stood beside him for a moment and drew the soft air into his lungs. He hadn't expected to do this again.

'Who's that?' Tommy sensed rather than saw the slim figure beside him.

'The Sub, sir, can I give you a spell?'

'Not for a while,' said Tommy, 'but you can help me to get an azimuth. I must check the compass. If this sky clears we should get a peek at the Pole star.'

'It looks to be clearing now,' said the Gannet.

'Good,' said Tommy and laughed softly. He was thinking that God must be very busy sorting out the requests for special weather. What the *Gauntlet* needed was half an hour's maximum visibility, followed by twelve hours of fog, followed by maximum visibility to enable her to make a successful rendezvous with *Goose*. Rather a tall order!

'Take a pencil and paper,' he said to the Gannet, 'and go aft to the compass. Write down the ship's head every time I say "Now". I'll get a bearing with the bridge "Pelorus". It's rough and ready but it'll have to do.'

Now it was the Gannet's turn to be shocked by the conditions below, and to marvel at the stoicism of the men who steered the submarine by sheer physical strength, in surroundings of all abiding danger.

He grinned at the two men who gave him back a weary nod and then explained what he was trying to do. Presently a faint voice from forward said: 'Ship's head – now!' He noted it down and waited.

For half an hour he repeated the process – Tommy was nothing if not patient in his navigation – and then, averaging the figures, returned to the bridge. The error worked out to be nearly fifteen degrees. 'Now we know where we are,' said Tommy, and left the Gannet while he went below to do some calculating on the chart.

By the time he'd finished it there was but one hour to dawn. Not worth turning in. The faithful Flunkey had managed to wake up and brew some hot tea. It was strong and sweet and very invigorating. Tommy thanked him and drank it slowly and gratefully. One hour until daylight, 'the condemned man made a hearty breakfast.'

CHAPTER SEVENTEEN

The dawn is overcast, the morning lowers,
And heavily in clouds brings on the day,
The great, the important day, big with – fate –

FOURTEEN men were out of action, but thanks to the fact that most of the *Gauntlet*'s machinery was in the same condition, there were enough men to man the guns, to drive the engine, and to steer the ship.

At half-past five that morning they were all at their stations, waiting to see what daylight would bring.

It was a black hour, the sea was quiet. An oily swell rocked the submarine gently and broke on her saddle tanks, making phosphorescent ripples round the hull. The air was warm and moisture-laden. It was difficult to know what sort of day it would be when the sun rose.

In this hour of waiting men spoke in low voices, stifled by yawns. There was nothing to do but wait. In all his experience in submarines Tommy had never before seen sunrise on the surface of the sea. It would be a new sensation; he hoped it wouldn't be the last time he was to experience it.

Down in the control-room Bill waited at the foot of the ladder; he had one advantage – he was able to smoke. He puffed thoughtfully at his cigarette and looked at Guts Hinton, who had joined him for a breath of air under the open hatch.

'Never knew a worser set-up than this,' said the coxswain. 'Not in all my experience. Did you, sir?'

'Looks a bit crafty,' said Bill, 'not to say dicey.'

' 'Ow long will the battery last, sir?'

'Another forty-eight hours, more or less.'

'And after that?'

Bill looked at him. 'Get out and walk,' he said.

'We might get picked up,' said the coxswain.

'Sure,' said Bill, 'we might.'

'What'll 'appen when we're run out of ammo?'

'Throw our boots at 'em,' said Bill.

'I must say,' said the coxswain, 'you take it all very calm, sir. Very calm indeed.'

'What the hell,' said Bill.

'Pity,' said Guts, 'she's a good old bitch: Lively on the after-planes. You can always tell a good sub by the way her arse comes up. Best divin' boat I ever knew. Was you ever in "L" boats?'

'Before my time,' said Bill.

'Cor, you didn't miss much. I was second-coxswain of one of 'em in China with Sanderson – you know, he's our *Captain S/M* now.'

'What was he like as a skipper?' asked Bill. He supposed he ought not to discuss his superiors with a Chief Petty Officer, but anything to pass the time.

'You'd 'ave laughed,' said Guts. 'That solemn. Never made a joke in 'is life. Not like our Tommy.' He cocked his thumb aloft. 'Never knew a better one than 'im. Did you, sir?'

'No,' said Bill, 'never.'

'Suppose he'll get into a packet o' trouble if we get back. He shouldn't oughter 'ave surfaced, should he, sir?'

'I don't suppose he'll care much, as long as he gets *us* back,' said Bill. 'He's not one of those ambitious chaps.'

'I remember 'im when he was a Sub-Lieutenant. That would 'ave been in the old second flotilla. Lively! Used to knock it back I can tell you. Every mornin' he'd come along to the 'swain (Skin-tight White, d'you remember 'im, sir?) and say: " 'Arf a gill please and plenty of milk," and he'd always get it. Did you good to see him laughing. He'll be a loss.'

'For Pete's sake, Hinton, don't talk about him as if he was dead.'

'We're all in the same boat, if you see what I mean,' said Guts. 'Might as well 'ave a bit of a natter seein' as we 'aven't long to live. Could *you* go 'arf a gill, sir? Quite a nip in the air. It'll put 'eart into you.'

'No,' said Bill. 'But I'll remind you of your offer *when* we get in.'

'You shall 'ave it. I'll be working up a nice surplus by then, now that two 'ave lost the numbers of their mess.'

'You're a rascal,' said Bill.

'Don't you believe it,' said the coxswain, 'I do what I

thinks right. That's all.'

'What about the regulations?'

'Like piecrust, made to be broken. Tell you what, isn't there a chance of pickin' up with one of our side?'

'There is a faint one. If we survive till dark.'

'Ah,' said the coxswain. 'That's it.' He held out his hand. 'Well,' he said, 'in case we're too busy, here's 'opin', sir. You and I always got on well together.' He turned to go and then turned back: 'Sure you don't want a tot? Can if you want to, you know.'

Bill smiled and shook his head, and the old ruffian started to go back to his job. You got close to men when things got dangerous. He looked up through the open hatch. It was still pitch dark. Mr Miles came forward; he hadn't left the engine-room all night and was grey with fatigue. Bill called his coxswain back and pointed to the Engineer Officer. Guts put his thumb up and went away to return with a noggin of rum.

'Dutch courage,' protested the Chief.

'Go on,' said the coxswain, 'it'll put 'eart into you.'

Mr Miles took it and drained it at a gulp. 'That's better,' he said. ''Ad me feet wet for rather a long time. Shouldn't be surprised if I didn't get piles. I've always been subject to 'em. Standin' in water's the worst possible thing for 'em. You'll see.'

'If that's the worst that happens to you,' said Bill, 'you can call yourself lucky.'

'Ah,' said the Chief, 'I was forgettin'. 'Ow's Oosit?' – this to the coxswain.

'Dead,' said the coxswain, 'didn't you know? Buried 'im this morning.'

'I'm sorry,' said the Chief, 'he was a good man.'

'They're all good men,' said Bill. 'You may borrow my sea-boots of you want to.'

'Thanks,' said Mr Miles, 'no point in riskin' another go. Very painful. We shall be busy when we get in.'

'Optimist,' said Bill.

He looked up the open hatch-way and saw that it was still pitch dark. The Skipper, he reflected, had got them up in plenty of time; not that he, Bill, had been asleep. Although darkness gave them complete safety he wished it would get light so that they would know the worst. This hanging about played Old Harry with the nerves. He walked forward to have a look at the wounded. They were a sick and sorry lot, suffering the inevitable reaction of the second day. The lightly wounded were helping their less fortunate friends. The compartment stank of disinfectant and other things, a smell which Bill would remember until his dying day.

'What's going on, sir?' whispered a seaman.

'It'll be light soon,' said Bill, 'then we shall see. How do you feel?'

'Not too bad, sir,' said the man. 'I've written a few lines to my missus. Will you take 'em, sir?'

'If you want me to, I will,' said Bill, 'but my chances are no better than yours, you know. It'll be all or nothing.'

'You never know,' said the seaman.

'Too right,' said Bill and took the letter, which he carefully folded and put in his breast pocket. 'I'll give this back to you when we get in,' he said cheerfully.

'That's right,' said the wounded man. He grinned painfully.

On deck the day was a long time coming. No one spoke now. They yawned a good deal, and those who had it chewed gum. Each man was thinking his own thoughts; getting himself conditioned to the inevitable. That was always the hard part; the acceptance of the situation. Once one had mastered the desire to go on hoping a new sort of serenity seemed to arrive and things looked less frightening.

Someone at the forward gun whistled tunelessly, the same air over and over again. Others began to follow suit until there was a chorus of desultory discords. Tommy had heard this tuneless whistling before, when he was on leave after Dunkirk, and he had stood on a station platform with hundreds of defeated and dispirited men who whistled without knowing it. Now his own crew had started this mournful indication of despair. What was being said now? 'Couldn't care less.' That was it.

'Stop that noise!' he said roughly. 'Lot of bloody canaries, you are. I can't hear anything.'

The whistling ceased; the seconds ticked very slowly and darkness seemed to be with them for all eternity.

He looked at the luminous dial of his watch. It was nearly sunrise, and yet so far there was no indication of it. Then, suddenly, even for this tropical zone, it started to get light. Here was no gradual lightening which crept up on one; it was as if some stage manager had switched on the first row of lights, and thereafter would go on switching on until the stage was fully illuminated.

'Like thunder, out of China 'cross the bay.' Tommy saw the point of that description for the first time. The black clouds silhouetted against a blood-red eastern sky. The sun was coming and throwing its rays upwards in traditional manner. 'Just like a bloody Japanese flag,' said Tommy. He climbed high up on the periscope fore-and-after and looked feverishly for evidence of searching surface craft, while the sun came out of the sea and cast an orange light along its surface before disappearing for good behind a black and lowering cloud. 'Came the dawn'; it was almost as quick as saying that.

With a tremendous sigh of relief Tommy became aware that there were no ships in sight. He had expected, and dreaded, the possibility of seeing a flotilla of small craft, spaced at intervals searching for the disabled submarine. Surely that was what any intelligent Admiral would have arranged. The chances of capturing a British submarine, and all that that implied, ought to have galvanised the enemy into sending out everything they'd got in the hopes that they would surprise the *Gauntlet* at dawn and prevent her from being scuttled. There could only be one reason for not sending out the searchers and that would be a fixed conviction that *Gauntlet* had already sunk, but surely the last aircraft to attack had seen that this was not the case! All the same it looked hopeful. No doubt the Japanese air force was not entirely convinced of its infallibility. No doubt patrolling aircraft would be sent out to the maximum range that the submarine could have reached in one night's steaming; no doubt one of them would see the *Gauntlet* and would wake up the hornets' nest anew, but all this would take time, and every hour would bring the *Gauntlet* nearer to her one chance of survival.

The minutes passed; the sun was mounting fast; it really was day now. There had been time for aircraft to take off in daylight and fly a hundred and fifty miles, but so far nothing had been heard or seen.

Slowly the spirits of the men on the bridge were undergoing a change. The calm and dispassionate expectation of annihilation was passing, and in its place a fervent hope was beginning to burgeon. It seemed impossible that their enemies could be able to act so stupidly. The Japanese were supposed to be so thorough. Little murmurs of conversation, an occasional laugh, combined with the relief of being once more able to smoke produced an atmosphere of restless gaiety. Hope was certainly springing in those breasts that fine morning in the Indian Ocean – but not for long.

It was, of course, Tommy who heard it first. A big four-engined job, it was. Flying high and purposefully on a westerly course. He saw glimpses of it through the clouds, and prayed that it would not come below them. Then, suddenly, it flew into a patch of clear sky, and all hope died in a moment.

They all could see her now and waited for her to turn and come in to attack, or at least to circle round while calling in the others, but she held on her course and disappeared to the westward, leaving everybody in a state of deep anxiety. Had she seen them? If not she would soon be returning from her search and might well pass right over them on the next journey. And so they were now pitchforked into a condition of mind as far removed from the early morning serenity born of despair, as it was possible to be. Twelve hours of daylight. It would never pass. It only needed two determined attacks completely to expend their remaining ammunition. Nobody would offer less than a hundred to one against their survival. Time was hardly moving for them.

The whistling broke out again. Tommy could not be bothered to check it. This inaction was killing. Time stood still.

CHAPTER EIGHTEEN

How could a day take so long to pass? How could it be that as one anxiety decreased another took its place?

Half-way through daylight Tommy had decided that the enemy would not come, unless there was a case of accidental sighting. Such a decision, one would have thought, would have given him nothing but a tremendous sense of relief. But not a bit of it. Now, the other circumstances began to swell in magnitude, until the situation, instead of looking more hopeful seemed to be almost hopeless, *unless*. . . .

It all now depended upon Mr Miles and his engines; if one of them could be kept running to give the *Gauntlet* a speed of six-and-a-half knots there would be just time for her to arrive at the rendezvous by midnight that night. If, of course, the rendezvous was not until another midnight, the *Gauntlet* must remain stopped, or cruising in the vicinity, rather than try to push on in the certain knowledge that the battery power was insufficient to keep the engine circulators going for the required distance. On the other hand, a chance encounter with one of his own side would become much more likely at a day's march nearer home; likewise another attack by enemy aircraft was always a possibility if he continued to hang about so close to their air-fields.

He sent for the signal and studied it carefully.

'*Goose will* sail – ' the operative word was '*will*'. When that signal was written by the Staff-Officer, *Goose* had not sailed, but that signal might have been written twenty-four hours before it went out on a routine transmission. Tommy sent for Toogood, who, greatly refreshed by a few hours' rest, was able to put his mind anew to the problem.

The chances were all in favour, he said, of *Goose* having sailed from Base at nineteen hundred last night. That being the case there was no possibility of her arriving at the rendezvous until the midnight *after next*. That was, of course, assuming that the signal which he (Toogood) had intercepted was a fresh one, and not a 'back general' pushed out as a matter of routine for just such a contingency as was occurring. In that case the 'time of origin' which is always tagged on to every message, would have cleared up the whole thing. Unfortunately the time of origin, which he had recorded, did not make sense. So there they were. On the whole the chances were 'midnight after next', but it wasn't certain.

'When's the next routine broadcast?' asked Tommy. Toogood told him. 'Can you rig up a listening circuit by then?'

'I'll try, sir.'

'Good. Take anything you want and any hands you want, and tell the First-Lieutenant to speak to me.'

'I'm here, sir,' said Bill, his voice preceding him up the conning-tower hatch.

'Ah,' said Tommy. 'How are the batteries?'

'Numbers one and two are getting pretty low,' said Bill. 'Number three is much higher because I've had the fuses broken since we found the chlorine.'

'All in all,' asked Tommy, 'how long can we rely on having juice?'

'Difficult to say,' said Bill. 'They die very quickly as the density drops.'

'Nothing definite anywhere. Will it last until tomorrow midnight?'

'Just about,' said Bill.

'It must,' said Tommy. 'Switch off everything, except one lamp in each compartment and as much as the Chief requires to keep the engine going.'

'And the battery fans,' added Bill, 'must keep them going, too much chlorine about.'

'Of course,' said Tommy, 'and pass the word that everything depends on economising in juice. What about number three battery – can we risk the chlorine?'

'If I could take the boards up,' said Bill, 'I'd bail out the cells with salt water in them, but I'd have to have some light to do it by, can't work in the dark.'

'We might be attacked at any moment,' said Tommy, 'but we'll have to risk it. Take some hands from the guns' crews and get cracking.'

Bill went below, full of energy, and glad to have a task of such magnitude.

Soon the control-room floor had been uprooted, and the

battery tops were exposed in all their ugliness. It was easy to see where the sea water had gone in. Half a dozen hands, employing squeeze bulbs began to draw off the offending liquid, squirting it into buckets which were once more hoisted up the hatch. Then fresh water from the drinking tanks was poured in and again drawn off; in that way little salt remained in the battery, though it stank to high heaven and would continue to do so as long as one particle remained.

While this was going on Mr Miles had his own worries to contend with. The water in the engine-room bilges was now getting low, and as it did so Mr Miles noticed a tendency for the crank-shaft bearings to warm up. It looked as if the bilge water was acting as a cooling agent. On the other hand its presence, where oil should be, was nothing if not bad. It seemed only a matter of time to him before the bearings fired up for the one reason or the other. He therefore set his available men to stripping the starboard engine in preparation for the fitting of a new piston. It was slow and back-breaking work, because the port engine's moving parts must be avoided if personal injury was not to be sustained, and every time he switched on another light Bill Brown's inquiring head would appear, as if by magic, in the doorway and ask if he couldn't do without it.

Up forward in the torpedo-room, Morgan Jones (aided by the coxswain) was dressing the wounds with more assurance on his part and a great deal more respect on the part of the coxswain. They were rapidly running out of clean bandages of any description, but then they were rapidly running out of everything, except perhaps danger.

As the moments slowly passed Tommy searched his mind for other matters which might help towards a successful issue out of all this affliction, and found precious little comfort. One alarming thought was, that since he had burned certain documents, he was now no longer in possession of the 'challenges' for the hour. This was printed on a special paper and had been, of course, included in the bonfire, for an enemy possessing the correct challenge would be able to spring an ambush. What would happen if they met *Goose*? Another worry. It wouldn't be the first time that friends had destroyed each other in time of war. And what would happen if *Goose* was not encountered? The sea is large and navigation by no means an accurate science. If he were three or four miles out in one direction and *Goose* a similar amount in another, they might never be close enough to sight each other's recognition signals.

Now the worries were coming thick and fast. Tommy sweated under their nagging presence and then pulled himself together. They'd never have got through so far if he'd taken an overall view of the situation at the out-set of this catastrophe. First things first. He sent for Morgan Jones and bade him do anything possible in the navigation line to ensure that *Gauntlet* would be in her correct position.

The last hours before darkness tried their nerves as nothing else had. Tempers were raw and the lack of hot food was making itself felt. The crew knew now that everything depended upon *which* midnight *Goose* was due. They saw the Captain's predicament and they didn't relish the thought of hanging about for twenty-four hours, instead of pressing on whilst their wasting assets were available. There was a certain amount of muttered conversation, and uninstructed criticism.

Meanwhile, Bert Toogood had accomplished the task of rigging up a small two-valve listening set and he was at the moment demonstrating it efficiency by listening to a short-wave transmission from the B.B.C. A soft and husky-voiced damsel was yelping in a manner that tugged at his heart-strings. She knew her job, did that crooner. 'I'll be seeing you,' she kept repeating. It was heart-rending. Her voice throbbed with pent-up feelings of nostalgia and suppressed desire. People had no right to push that sort of stuff out, reflected Bert; if he went on listening to it he wouldn't have the strength of mind to do more than think of home and a fat lot of good that was in his present case. He switched it off angrily and tuned carefully on the *Carpentaria*'s wavelength, though it yet lacked a quarter of an hour to the routine broadcast. Then he weakened and turned back the dial until once more the siren's voice came thinly through his ear-phones. His mate caught the sound of it, and sighed deeply.

'Cor,' he said, 'she puts me in mind of that bint in Alex, remember her? Talk about dark-eyed beauties – cor!' He sighed. 'Turn it up – you're makin' me cry.'

Bert grinned and switched off. He wasn't the only one she did things to. 'Favourite of the Forces' was she? She'd find out one day if she wasn't careful. He balanced a signal pad on his knee and adjusted his tuning with great concentration. Soon he heard the *Carpentaria* come on the air and then suddenly she started to send.

She was calling *Gauntlet,* or rather she was addressing herself to *Gauntlet,* and expected no reply. She would repeat the message when darkness came. Something like nostalgia came once more to Bert. He knew the 'Sparker' in the *Carpentaria.* He could see him, cigarette drooping from his lips, a photo of Betty Grable by his transmitting key and some curiously effeminate paper lace decorating his desk. He was a great one for making paper lace; it took hours of snipping and folding and the result, though ingenious was not to Bert's liking. Still, the Sparker liked it. Curious how one could read morse at that speed and yet think one's own thoughts. Sparker was certainly peeling it out tonight pretty fast, but Bert could take it. Ah! Over run himself then. 'Repeat last group,' too much thought of Betty Grable.

Page after page of figures, all neatly written in five-letter groups. That lot would take close on an hour to decipher. Wordy lot the *Carpentaria,* sendin' out all that stuff and little of it of any value to a patrolling submarine. Presently it ended, and *Carpentaria* went off with a click. Gingerly Bert tuned back in search of the husky voiced crooner but she had finished and in her place a man was telling a funny story against a background of hysterical applause.

Bert turned over the earphones to his mate and went forward to the wardroom where he knew the Gannet would help with the deciphering.

For half an hour they worked until nothing was left undone. Then, and only then, did Bert dare to comprehend the purport of all the messages. There was one for *Gauntlet,* instructing her to shift her position for the last week of her patrol; there was another to *Goose,* giving similar instructions. That proved that *Goose* was at sea. He turned back to look for the Time of Origin and found the clue that he had been hoping for. From its time and date it was clear that *Goose* had sailed nearly forty-eight hours ago. That meant that she would reach the rendezvous at midnight tonight! He went quickly on to the bridge to put his Captain's mind at rest.

CHAPTER NINETEEN

THE plan for what the Americans like to call 'meeting up with' the *Goose* was a simple enough one. On arrival in position Tommy intended to fire recognition lights from a 'Very' pistol at intervals of a quarter of an hour throughout the night, or until their stock of cartridges was exhausted. There was nothing else he could do.

Of course, such an action was fraught with dangerous consequences; a Japanese patrol might be the first to turn up – that was a risk which must be accepted. As a secondary precaution Tommy decided to keep back a dozen signal cartridges, in case this was not the right midnight after all.

When darkness fell all thoughts on board centred upon this chance of meeting *Goose*. Everybody knew the situation, though no organised 'hand-out' of news existed aboard. In a submarine the grape-vine works very well. The Captain states his intentions to his officers, and those who are near it are included in the broadcast. If the Captain wishes to keep a secret, he tells no one, for that is the only way that secrets can be kept.

Tommy had had thoughts of gathering his crew together, and giving them a few well-chosen words of encouragement. He probably would have done so if it had not been that he had recently seen a film of naval action in which the Captain fell in his crew every time the bell struck, and admonished them in the manner of the fifth form of St Dominic's. This mass objurgation was probably a good thing in a big ship, within moderation; it gave the humbler members of the crew a feeling of being in the know; but here, there were no humbler members, and there would be, therefore, only one reason for calling a meeting; to say good-bye and to thank them. Such a course was unthinkable; therefore, no oratory.

Up on the bridge the Captain peered into the darkness and wondered whether he should not start popping the signal lights off at an earlier hour than that of the rendezvous.

Behind him the leading signalman, one Jago, who had hitherto played a very small part in this narrative, fingered his pistol and touched and retouched the cartridges. A signalman on patrol has little opportunity to perform his specialised duties; he just acts as a look-out, takes a trick at the hydroplanes and generally mucks in with the seamen; but when the operation is over, and the tired submarine approaches her base, he comes into his own, and it's 'Signalman on the bridge!' day and night.

At eleven o'clock that evening Tommy's patience was exhausted. He closed up all gun's crews, warned them not to open fire without orders, and turned to Jago. 'Go on,' he said.

'What shall we give 'em, sir?' asked Jago.

'Got any blue ones?'

'No, sir, green.'

'Then we can't be patriotic. Give 'em red, white and green, exactly every quarter of an hour. Got it?'

'Yes, sir. Red, white and green.'

'O.K. Carry on.'

Phut! Phut! Phut!

A little burst of flame and smoke at the pistol point, a few seconds' wait and then a single colour star from each cartridge, floating down gracefully to quench itself in the sea. Fifteen seconds of hope, followed by fifteen minutes of waiting.

Supposing *Goose* was in the vicinity, what would she make of this random selection of coloured lights? Many a time on patrol Tommy had sighted odd lights, which never explained their presence, but never had he permitted curiosity to triumph over natural caution. The chap who minded his own business in war time might live to see the peace. That was the reason why he instructed the signalman to fire the lights *exactly* at each quarter of an hour. He hoped, thereby, to rouse the curiosity of Shiner Wright, for he knew his man. Shiner would notice the regular feature of the fireworks. He might say that this was obviously an enemy preconceived plan to signal to a consort, in which case he might well investigate it in the hopes of bagging something. Even if he didn't the steady persistence and regularity of the lights would nag him into some action or other. Shiner was an active body, and took some long chances from time to time. It was he who had wandered into a harbour in the Aegean and had touched off everything in sight, disappearing in the smoke to collect a well-merited gong. Shiner would join in any dog fight. Tommy was pretty confident of attracting his attention, provided always that he was there.

Phut! Phut! Phut! Eleven-fifteen p.m. The stars fell close alongside and they heard the finality of that hiss as the sea quenched them. Tommy turned to the signalman; might as well be hanged for a sheep. 'Got your Aldis lamp?' he asked.

'All ready, sir.'

'Right,' said Tommy. 'Get up on the standard and flash SOS every forty-five degrees round the horizon.'

'Aye, aye, sir.'

Flick-flick-flick, flack-flack-flack, flick-flick-flick. The pale pencil of light started out bravely enough but the beam seemed to disappear into the haze within a few dozen yards.

A man at the gun gave an exclamation.

'What is it?' asked Tommy.

'There, sir – a light,' said the man.

'Don't say "there",' expostulated Tommy, in his mildest voice. 'Give me a bearing.'

'Red fifty, sir,' said the man. 'I could 'ave sworn I saw something.'

They watched on that bearing, and the signalman kept his lamp flickering upon it, but not one of them saw anything. Then another man saw another light, which turned out to be a glimpse of the new moon, as it rose behind the clouds. Tommy cautioned them not to cry wolf, and not to report anything until two men had seen the same light at the same time.

Phut! Phut! Phut!

Eleven-thirty. Now there really was a chance. Half-an-hour's steaming was only five miles. It was an overwhelmingly exciting thought, that suddenly out of the teeming darkness, safety would come. It didn't bear thinking about.

Something splashed on to Tommy's hand – a rain-drop – the first of a downpour, which came and blotted out the whole world. The poor little beam of the Aldis lamp flickered feebly into a wall of tropical rain. It was useless to fire the Very lights; visibility was not more than a quarter of a mile. The men at the guns cursed, the signalman continued to flick-flick, until Tommy told him to pack it up. They stood in the rain and felt their chances disappearing.

'Midnight, sir,' said the signalman.

'No good,' said Tommy, 'better save it for a fine patch.' Pray God Shiner would be late! People seldom looked behind them. If Shiner was up to time he might now be within a mile of them. Tommy changed his mind.

'As you were! Give 'em a burst for luck. You never know!'

Phut! Phut! Phut!

Poor little stars, only just visible from the bridge. 'SOS' went the Aldis.

'This bloody rain's cooked our flaming goose,' said Tommy in a low voice to Bill who had come up to see how things were going. 'Not a hope of seeing us in this.' It was the first note of despondency that the Captain had allowed to creep into his voice.

'I think it's easing a bit, sir,' said Bill, more to soothe the savage breast than anything else.

'Easing my aunt fanny,' said Tommy rudely: then, 'I do believe you're right! Give her another burst, Jago!'

Gone was the methodical approach. This was the end of the tether. It was now, or never!

'And another one,' said Tommy. Something was urging him to give everything he had at this moment.

'Now, shine your Aldis right ahead and keep flicking.' Near breaking point now. Why was he so excited? 'Go on, man, what's the matter?'

'It's clearing,' said Bill, as indeed it was.

Tommy seized the pistol and fired another trio. Then he swung himself upwards into the periscope fore-and-after and stared out ahead. 'I must keep calm,' he told himself. 'This is no way for a Captain to behave. I must keep calm.' Was that something ahead? A pinpoint of light? He abandoned all sense of self-preservation and raised his glasses with both hands. The *Gauntlet* lurched. He grabbed at something, missed it and fell heavily on to his First-Lieutenant.

'Are you all right, sir?' Bill's voice was muffled, but not so muffled as Tommy's, who had nearly knocked himself out on the handle of the engine-room telegraph.

'Right ahead,' he said distantly, 'right ahead.'

Then the crew took it up. 'There she is, sir! That's 'er all right! See 'er, Bunts? Go on, answer 'im.'

Discipline was near to breaking.

Bill jumped up and took charge. 'Silence,' he ordered.

'Are you reading him, Jago?'

'Not yet, sir,' said the signalman, 'he's too far off.'

'Go on flashing,' said Bill. 'How are you, sir?' This to the Captain.

Tommy was in no condition to speak. All the stars that ever issued from a Very's cartridge were spinning before his eyes, to all intents and purposes he was flat out. He held on to the bridge whilst it spun round him, and then he felt sick.

'Here, sir,' said Morgan Jones, 'this'll clear your head.'

The sal volatile did the trick – the world ceased to spin and his memory began to return. Something had happened just as he had fallen. Bill dropped alongside him, anxious to know whether he should take command or not. Moments, precious moments, were fleeting, the crew was whispering.

'How are you, sir?'

'I thought I saw a light,' said Tommy vaguely, 'and then I lost my balance.'

'It was a light,' said Bill, 'it still is.'

'What's he making?' he called the signalman.

'N. C. B.,' read out Jago, as the letters flickered through the darkness.

'The challenge,' said Bill, 'and we can't answer it.'

Tommy's brain was clearing; he had foreseen this. 'Make to him,' he said, 'this is *Gauntlet.*'

Flick-flick went the lamp. '*Gauntlet,*' repeated the signalman. 'Badly damaged with casualties aboard,' went on Tommy. His head was splitting but he could think all right.

' – aboard,' concluded the signalman.

'Please close me.'

'He may not be *Goose,*' said Bill.

'Too late now,' said Tommy.

The signalman began to sing out a message he was reading.

'Why don't you answer my challenge?'

English, thank God! Shiner wasn't sticking his neck out.

'All burnt,' said Tommy.

'Message passed,' said Jago.

There was a pause. The stranger's light had gone out. Shiner, if it was Shiner, was thinking. In spite of his intense feelings of pain and excitement Tommy had a momentary glimpse of his pal in a characteristic attitude. Scratching his head and saying: 'That's a crafty one, how do I know he isn't a bloody Nip?'

' 'E's bobbin' at you, Bunts,' said a helpful member of the gun's crew. Jago swallowed a snarl and started to read.

'What ship?' he sang out.

'*Gauntlet,* pendants G four two,' instructed Tommy.

Flick-flick-flick – went the Aldis.

'Message passed,' said Jago.

' 'E's bobbin',' said the helpful man.

'For crying out loud,' said Jago. 'I'm not bloody well blind!'

'What is the name of the commanding officer's wife?'

'Good old Shiner,' said Tommy. 'I wouldn't have thought it of you. Audrey,' he called.

' 'Ow d'you spell it, sir?'

Tommy told him. Audrey! He never had expected to use such a word again. Audrey, with that sound burst the full realisation that the worst was over. 'Add to Audrey, who are you?'

'*Goose.*'

At last!

Then the gun's crew burst the bounds of discipline. They cheered and slapped each other on the back.

Tommy went to the voice-pipe. 'Control-room!' he called.

It was Mr Miles who answered. 'Chief here, sir.'

'Oh Chief,' said Tommy, 'we've made contact with *Goose*. Pass the word, will you?'

'Aye, aye, sir,' said Mr Miles, 'just as well, sir,' he added, 'I was just coming up to tell you that we'll 'ave to stop the engine, after thrust is red-'ot!'

CHAPTER TWENTY

No longer alone. No longer isolated from the outside world. Everyone aboard the *Gauntlet* now understood the meaning of the expression – 'a new lease of life'; but it still remained problematical as to how long the new lease would turn out to be.

It depended upon the outcome of next day's enemy activity and whether Mr Miles could coax one of his engines into new life.

In the meantime the feeling of relief was profound. Shiner Wright, in the *Goose*, wasted no time in closing the *Gauntlet* until the two vessels were heaving on adjacent swells. Then with the aid of the megaphones the two Captains conversed. Shiner opened it in characteristic fashion:

'What's the matter,' he bellowed.

Tommy condensed the last hundred pages of this narrative into a few sentences.

'You have had a rousing time,' said Shiner. 'I'll send my First-Lieutenant over in the boat. What do you most want?'

'Bandages, morphia and electric torches,' said Tommy.

'Any bods?' asked Shiner.

Tommy thought of his worn-out men, and the necessity of incessant pumping to clear the ship of water; if he could give them a hot meal and a few hours' sleep they would be able to carry on almost indefinitely. 'Can you spare me half a dozen,' he said, 'just for the time being? I want to rest my chaps.'

'Do you think you can get her in?' asked Shiner.

'I'm going to get her in,' said Tommy, 'but I'll have to have a tow most of the way, if not all.'

'I'll get on the blower,' said Shiner, 'and tell old man Sanderson to send out a rescue party. How's that?'

'Fine,' said Tommy.

Presently Toogood called up the voice-pipe and read out

the signal which he had intercepted from *Goose*'s transmission.

'Goose to Captain S/M, Carpentaria,' it ran, 'am in company with *Gauntlet* badly damaged, unable to dive, fourteen casualties. Both engines and motors out of action. Will stand by her until further orders. *Gauntlet* hopes to get one engine going shortly, but doubtful if battery will last. Will need a tow. My position (etc., etc., etc.,).'

Meanwhile the flickering of lights on *Goose*'s casing gave evidence of activity in connection with the assembling and launching of her collapsible boat, and very soon the frail little craft was rowed across the heaving waters and disembarked three men with stores. Then it went back for more. Peter Jackman, the *Goose*'s First-Lieutenant, was the first to arrive on the bridge. Tommy took him below and gave him a personally conducted tour of the vessel. Jackman's face reflected his feelings as he saw the state of affairs, and his eyes opened their widest as he saw the water still swishing over the floor plates of the engine-room, and the weary pumping party still at the job of reducing the level. He blanched a bit, too, at the sights in the torpedo-room and he was a very thoughtful man as he sat down in the little wardroom and made notes of the names of casualties, including, of course, the two dead men. Tommy felt sorry for him; such an exhibition was not a good preparation for a patrol in enemy waters. As soon as he could he sent the young officer back to his own ship and went into the engine-room to make encouraging noises at Mr Miles.

With both engines stopped the shipping of a new piston to one of them and the reconnection of the circulating pump for its normal function, became a speedier operation.

Izzy Sammons and his team of quiet-mannered artificers, worked like men possessed. Forward, Morgan Jones and the coxswain re-dressed all the wounds with new bandages, and were able to give relief to the men in pain. All along the ship a satisfying smell of hot pastry was fighting with, and overpowering, the acrid stink of chlorine, for Tommy had removed the ban on cooking for one good meal and the cooks were taking full advantage of it. Once more the cheerful clatter of cooking utensils sounded in the messes. Appetites, which trepidation had kept in subjection, now assumed gigantic proportions. It was not before 3 a.m. that the meals were cooked and eaten and thereafter the weary men dropped where they were and slept.

Bill Brown, walking through the ship, alert for any sign of an increase of chlorine, looked at the sleeping figures, some huddled, some stretched out in the gangway, some with their heads fallen on to their plates, and saw how near a thing it had been to disaster. A few more hours and their resources would have been completely exhausted.

Even now it wasn't over by a long chalk. Another day would dawn soon and they were still far from home.

The Gannet, now exhibiting definite signs of recovering his lost reputation as a trencherman, was keeping watch on the bridge. Tommy could not tear himself away from the engine-room where he watched the men at work, and talked quietly to Mr Miles, while down in the bilges the hand pump clanked wearily. The *Goose*'s men were finding it harder going than the men who had worked because their lives depended upon it.

By five o'clock the engine was ready for a trial. Tommy went on the bridge and flashed a signal to *Goose* who had withdrawn to a greater distance. He was senior to Shiner Wright by about a fortnight, and this entitled him to give the orders. Then he wound the engine-room telegraph and waited.

To his great joy the engine started up and proceeded to settle down to a steady rhythm which sounded healthy enough. Away on the beam an invisible *Goose* was steering a parallel course. The withdrawal was proceeding, 'according to plan'.

Tommy, by now, had gone past the stage where he needed sleep. His mind was too active for sleep. He couldn't get used to the idea of life with a future to it, and of Audrey, whom he had never expected to see again, and there was another aspect of the future which wasn't so bright.

He would be called to account for this sorry state of affairs when he got in. That did not unduly perturb him, he had done what he considered to be right and was quite prepared to take the consequences, but he would be very sorry indeed if this fracas meant the breaking up of his magnificent ship's-company. *Gauntlet* would need a long refit; her crew couldn't hang about waiting for her to be mended; that meant that they would be drafted to 'spare crew' and dispersed. As for the officers, they, too, would kick their heels in the depot-ship until vacancies, due to decease or promotion, moved them into other vessels. This then meant the end, either way. Tommy was sorry.

'Captain, sir.' It was Toogood with another signal.

'*Goose* from *Carpentaria*,' it ran, 'remain in company with *Gauntlet* until joined by *Wolfcub* who should reach you by fifteen-thirty hours today.'

Now they really were going to be saved. Tommy ought to have been greatly relieved. If he was, he didn't feel it. Perhaps because he was so tired, perhaps because in the past days he had been living so intensely in his tiny world, completely apart from the rest of humanity. Now, he must go back to a life full of senior officers, despatches, reports – and possibly courts-martial. The future loomed large with troubles of all sorts. Perhaps it would have been simpler if one of those bombs had been a fraction nearer? Tommy was tired.

Half an hour before sunrise a weary crew stood to. They didn't expect a dawn surprise, but, on the other hand, they had been advertising their presence with light and some chance patrol vessel might well have sighted something. So they yawned and nattered in low voices, and waited for daylight to allow them to go below and rest again.

It was a mirror calm morning, airless, and heavily overcast. The barograph, which continued to tick merrily, and was one of the few going concerns aboard, showed a considerable fall in barometric pressure.

'Lots of wind coming,' said Tommy, 'good job it didn't come sooner.' Come to think of it, they had been lucky, dead lucky. Would it hold?

Daylight arrived with all its dramatic suddenness, and showed a completely empty horizon, though not a very distant one. Of *Goose* there was no sign. Shiner wouldn't have done otherwise than dive before dawn; he was somewhere around, exercising his crew and making arrangements to manage with six men under his proper complement. He'd be popping up soon.

'Fall out the guns' crews, sir?' asked Bill.

'Yes, please,' said Tommy.

'Periscope on the port bow!'

'Hold on,' said Tommy. Of course it was only *Goose*, but you couldn't be too careful.

'Gone now, sir,' said the signalman.

Tommy put his glasses to his eyes, and watched the surface of the water. Presently he saw a quiver and a ripple on the surface and then, out of the depths a thin stick protruded, turning this way and that like the music-hall definition of a peninsula, 'A long neck looking out to see.' And then the one periscope was joined by another and fatter one. That settled it – she was a friend, and was showing herself without any attempt to avoid detection. They watched, with all the professional interest of their trade, to see the antics of their flotilla-mate. It wasn't often that one got the chance to see a submarine in action at such close range.

'Fall out the guns' crews,' said Tommy, 'that's *Goose* all right.'

But nobody moved. They watched the periscopes with interest; now they were close on the beam and moving at speed, throwing up two fine white feathers of spray.

'He's going to do gun-action surface,' said Bill.

'Bet he mucks it,' said the Gannet hopefully. 'There he goes.' As he spoke the two periscopes leaned forward and slid out of sight. Nothing remained visible save a few white bubbles and a slight swirl from the *Goose*'s rapidly turning propellers. They'd all seen this before, but loved to watch; there was something fascinating at the thought of that great steel cigar, capable of moving in three dimensions; and, of course, they were able to imagine exactly what was going on inside her.

At this moment, no doubt, the guns' crews were crouching in the access towers, waiting for the rapid surfacing of the submarine.

'Come on,' said Tommy; he yawned. 'Ought to be up by now.'

'There she blows,' said Bill.

It was indeed like the surfacing of some great fish. First the tip of one periscope, then the curved extremity of her streamlined bow. Then suddenly the whole upper part came out of the water at tremendous speed. Water gushed from her freeing-ports in great silver gouts. White foam bubbled round the base of her conning-tower, but as yet there was no sign of life aboard her. Then, as if they had been ejected by springs, the men were everywhere. Round went the guns and the voices of the loaders came over the water. 'Ready!'

'Not bad,' said Bill 'a bit slow with the training of the gun.'

'Too much angle,' said Tommy, 'for my liking. Gives you away at least fifteen seconds before you can open up. Much better do a flatter surface. Don't you agree, coxswain?'

Guts Hinton nodded. 'Yes, sir,' he said, 'take the angle off at twenty-five feet is what we used to say. Nothin' 'll stop 'er from coming up after that. Makes it easier for the gun's crew too.'

'How was it?' called Shiner through his megaphone.

'Lousy,' answered Tommy.

'Jealous,' shouted Shiner. He had something there.

A burst of smoke at *Goose*'s tail showed that she was now on her Diesel engines. Gradually she crept close alongside until Tommy was compelled to expostulate.

'I'm hand-steering from aft,' he called, 'we don't want to bump at this stage.'

'O.K.' said Shiner. 'Listen. If we sight anything on the surface I'll "*plonger vite*" and try to nobble them while you act like a wounded stag. O.K.?'

'Sure,' said Tommy. 'We'll have to take our chance with aircraft too. Don't stay up: One punctured hull is enough.'

'In that case,' said Shiner, 'you better have some of my ammo. You can't shoot without bullets.'

'All right,' said Tommy. 'If you think it's safe to stop.'

'I'll get everything ready,' called Shiner as he sheered off, 'and when we are, you stop and I'll come alongside – there's practically no swell and we won't bump each other – much.'

And so it turned out. The two vessels came gently together and boxes of ammunition were passed by hand across their saddle tanks. Every man aboard each vessel was employed and the whole operation took less than five minutes. At the same time Tommy surrendered the six men who had kept the pump going during the night watches. They departed willingly enough; the atmosphere of chlorine and disinfectant had not appealed to them.

Half an hour later the two submarines set course again for a rendezvous with *Wolfcub*, one mile apart abeam. It really looked as if their luck was holding.

CHAPTER TWENTY-ONE

ONLY three hours remained of daylight and only two before the rendezvous would be reached. The barometer continued to fall and the air to become more and more oppressive. It would be as well to effect a junction with the destroyer as soon as possible and to transfer the wounded before the storm, which was so obviously brewing, burst upon them.

Down below Mr Miles and Bill were in anxious confabulation.

'She's leaking somewhere else,' said the Chief. 'Stands to reason. The amount of pumping that's been going on should 'ave cleared the ship hours ago, and yet it looks to me as if there's more water in the bilges now than there was last night.'

'It's not coming through that patch,' said Bill. 'Are you sure someone hasn't left something open?'

Mr Miles gave him a pitying glance. 'We're not seamen.' he said, 'we know which way to turn a valve-handle. Not like some I know of.'

'Then what is it? asked Bill.

'Fractured pipe as like as not,' said the Chief. 'Some of them crumps was a bit too close for comfort.' He sighed. 'If it comes up much higher it'll be over the top of my sea-boots.'

'*My* sea boots,' said Bill.

'And then,' said Mr Miles, 'I'll 'ave wet feet again.'

'Shall I tell the Skipper?' asked Bill.

'I'll 'ave another looksee first,' said the Chief. 'I've got an idea where the trouble might be.'

They separated and Bill went back to the wardroom, where Tommy at last had turned in on his bunk. The entire submarine was in darkness save for one lamp in each compartment. Even with this rigid economy the battery densities were dropping at an alarming speed. It showed by the dimness of the filaments in the few lights which were switched on. Bill looked at his watch. In three hours they'd be out of the worst of it.

On the bridge the Gannet rejoiced in his new-found health. His pains were not forgotten, in fact he remembered them with feelings of wonder that he was now so comfortable. He stood on the bridge chatting with the look-out. It was afternoon, and a sleepy one at that. Enemy action was now such a thing of the past that with the Captain sleeping below a state of relaxation had spread everywhere. After all, in three hours' time they would be safely under the wing of a surface vessel. *Goose* was better than nothing, but she couldn't have towed them, or communicate by boat, unless this flat calm continued, which it was not going to. Come darkness and they would be as much out of danger as was possible in war time.

Down below Tommy's subconscious mind was at work on him, nagging at him for resting. It took the form of a dream of extraordinary reality. A destroyer was in sight – it was *Wolfcub* of course – but it wasn't! It was a Japanese one – all was lost!

He woke up, sweating with fear, and went straight up on the bridge, half expecting to find a Japanese naval officer on watch. All was quiet. He lit a cigarette and reproached himself for being windy. Reaction, he supposed. They had had a bit of a time in these last few days. Audrey! What a lot he'd have to tell her when they got in. It wouldn't have done to have gone so soon after George Carter. Poor Audrey; men must work and women must weep. Just as true in this war as any other one, even though half the women were dressed in uniform. Of course there were air-raids, and all that, but men had the best of it, no doubt about that. Fancy sitting ashore when the girl you love was off on some dangerous operation. Not likely!

'What?'

The Sub had said something under his breath.

'Did you speak?'

'Would you have a look, sir?'

'What is it?'

'On the starboard quarter – I think it's a ship.'

Tommy levelled his glasses for a while and then he spoke rapidly. 'Gun action stations!' he ordered. 'Signalman! Call up *Goose* and make: "Enemy destroyer to the south-westward." '

Goose was not caught napping. She dived before the signalman had time to call her up. Tommy altered course away from the approaching destroyer and called for full speed from Mr Miles. Everything depended now upon *Goose*; every minute extra before the Japanese destroyer opened fire would help her to get in for a close torpedo attack. Shiner must be in a proper stew. If he missed his attack that would be the end of *Gauntlet*, and everybody in her. What had he said? Act like a wounded stag? Put a list on the ship and show no aggressive spirit? Hoist a white flag and lure the enemy into the trap? It was common sense to do this but he wasn't going to do it. A nice debatable point that. Was it justifiable to hold up your hands in surrender and then push a bayonet into the unsuspecting victim's guts? But after all, the days of cricket were past: those yellow-bellies gave no quarter and expected none. Why not line up the crew on deck, put an angle on the ship and hang out a white flag? Think of the wounded, it would probably save all their lives. And where's the harm?

The enemy was about seven miles off coming in on a regular zig-zag. It was difficult to know whether they had sighted the *Gauntlet*, so deliberate were their movements.

At the speed they were going the whole thing would be over in a quarter of an hour. If *Goose* didn't fire within ten minutes it would be all up.

It was an extraordinary situation to be in; to be obliged to creep along the surface of the calm sea, while the enemy came for them, and somewhere between them Shiner was sweating blood to get into point-blank range. The three-inch gun's crew loaded their weapon and trained it as far as it would bear, but Tommy bade them train it back again. He was fighting a battle with his traditional training. A white flag as a *ruse de guerre*. Was it justifiable?

Steadily the destroyer closed them. Five minutes to the deadline. Now it was clear that the enemy was not a chance encounter, but one sent out to look for *Gauntlet*. That being the case she ought to find what she was looking for, a badly damaged submarine with a heavy list, and a despairing crew. Quickly flooding the port tanks and ordering some of the men to run about the casing in simulated panic, Tommy turned to the voice-pipe, to order a white flag to be provided. He opened his mouth but somehow could not say it. Three minutes to the deadline; he'd give himself till then and then, if Shiner had not done his stuff he would pocket his pride and lower himself to the level of his enemy.

Judging by the bearing of the enemy and the position that Shiner had been in it ought to be a snip for a short-range attack. The enemy was employing a simple zig-zag and the attacker was aware that eventually the destroyer would come close to *Gauntlet*. The trouble was that there was very little time; with an enemy moving at that speed a few seconds' delay and the torpedoes would miss. Shiner was obviously in a quandary, whether to wait and get a sitting bird for certain, or to fire at the first opportunity. If he delayed the Japanese might blow *Gauntlet* out of the water, though it certainly looked as if they were out to capture her intact.

'She's opened fire,' said the Gannet, and had to steel himself against a desire to drop flat on his face. At that range they couldn't miss.

Three splashes dead ahead showed that this was the traditional shot across the bows.

'Stop Port!' ordered Tommy. His voice was dry and detached. 'Get a white flag up!' They looked at him.

'A white flag, sir?' said Jago.

'You heard what I said,' said Tommy.

'We haven't got one, sir,' said Jago.

'Of course you haven't,' said Tommy, 'get a table cloth, or a sheet, or any bloody thing.' Shiner was expecting him to play his part that was clear.

They were being very stupid about the white flag, apparently there wasn't anything white on board.

'Call him up – with the Aldis,' said Tommy.

'What shall I say?' asked Jago.

'Anything you can think of to keep him guessing,' said Tommy. 'And stand by to go ahead on the engine.'

He didn't like the situation at all, the destroyer was coming up fast; if Shiner didn't fire soon the *Gauntlet* would be in the line of sight. 'Come on, Shiner, for God's sake.'

She was a big modern ship. All her guns were trained upon the *Gauntlet*. One little word, and that would be the end.

'Make "Help!" to him,' said Tommy. 'Where's that white flag?'

But it was no good, there just wasn't one to be found. Tommy had a sudden thought of the twelve wounded men, waiting helplessly for the end. He must do everything possible for them. His shirt was white – at least it had been. He started to pull it over his head when suddenly the thing happened.

Four almost simultaneous gouts of fire and water rose above the enemy. They were followed by a rumbling explosion which split her in half and turned her over. For a moment her bottom was upright and her propellers whirring madly in the air, then a dense pall of black smoke hid her from view and when it lifted the ship was gone. Shiner had not failed.

The magnitude of the disaster which had overtaken the ship was such that the watchers forgot their own case – that they had been saved and that their enemy had been destroyed. They just could not take it in.

Tommy tucked his shirt in and found his knees to be trembling. He, too, was stunned by this sudden horrid disintegration that he had witnessed. At the back of his mind, however, there was one small clear patch which registered satisfaction; satisfaction that he had not actually shown the white flag.

CHAPTER TWENTY-TWO

LEAVING *Goose* to surface and search the area for survivors, Tommy set course for the rendezvous at his best speed. He had good reasons for doing this, for since he could not go astern with his propellers his vessel was not well suited for any rescue work which might be necessary. His main reason, however, was that charity begins at home. He had on board twelve wounded men, some of them seriously ill, and he wanted to get them out of the *Gauntlet* before the weather broke, as break it was going to. The problem of getting injured men out of the submarine would be greatly eased if the fore-hatch could be opened, and that would only be possible in the flattest of calms. Yet another reason for scurrying away from that scene of awe-inspiring destruction was the possibility of retaliation. The Japanese destroyer would not have had time to make any sort of signal *after* the torpedoes had exploded with such completely devastating effect, but she might well have been in contact with her base at the time of it, and the sudden and inexplicable cessation of all further communications might well result in the despatch of reinforcements. The absence of aircraft was explained by the low ceiling of cloud which hung heavily only a few hundred feet overhead. Even so, it was quite likely that any suspicion of hostile activity would result in a fresh eruption from the hornet's nest. Therefore the best policy was to get away while the going was good.

As for the weather, the line which the pen was drawing on the barograph was the steepest that Tommy had ever seen. A cyclone was coming, no doubt at all about it, and when it did come it would effectively put a stop, both to enemy action, and to any rescue operations. To get the wounded out before it broke upon them was of paramount importance.

It was with the greatest relief that Tommy sighted the *Wolfcub* and was able to signal his requirements to her.

She put up a good exhibition of seamanship, coming up from astern of the *Gauntlet,* dropping her sea-boat, so that it sheered across the intervening gap of water with hardly more than a few strokes from the rowers. Then she circled round and by the time the whaler was loaded with men, she was back alongside to pick them up.

The first to step on board the *Gauntlet* was a two-striped doctor, who showed by every action of his that he was on the job. He gave Tommy a perfunctory salute and disappeared below to examine the wounded. Morgan Jones and the coxwain had worked together to smarten up the general appearance of the injured men, as far as possible, and the young doctor, when he saw the bandaging, looked quickly round to see who was responsible for it.

'Did you do this?' he asked Guts. The coxswain hesitated between speaking the truth and taking all the credit to himself, and then, for reasons of his own, he conceded a point to his rival.

'Me and Mr Jones,' he said.

The young doctor looked round and recognised Morgan Jones. 'So it's you,' he said, 'I thought that there was a bit more than qualified-in-first-aid in the dressing of these wounds.'

Morgan Jones smiled. 'Seems that my profession has caught up with me,' he said.

'Does that mean you're coming back to us?' asked the doctor.

Morgan Jones nodded.

'Don't blame you,' said the young doctor, with blundering frankness. 'Once of this sort of thing would be quite enough for me too.'

Morgan Jones bit his lip. From now on it would always be assumed that he had run away from submarines to hospital because he'd had a beating-up at sea. That was the price he would always have to pay for having gone to sea to escape hospital. Funny, that!

Four journeys were necessary, for the serious cases had to be stretched out across the thwarts. The actual handling of the stretchers, from the upper-deck casing of the submarine to the whaler which heaved in the steadily increasing swell, was an exhausting operation for all concerned; moreover, the sight of the wounded in day-light was distressing enough. The sea-boat's crew of the *Wolfcub* could barely dare to look at the gaunt and filthy men who had endured so much. That they were deeply impressed was borne out by the fact that the young officer in charge of the sea-boat was seen to leave his boat and climb to the *Wolfcub*'s bridge. Shortly afterwards the destroyer's loud hailer began to speak.

'*Gauntlet* ahoy!' said a stentorian voice. Tommy raised an arm. 'There's a cyclone warning. It's due very soon.'

Tommy again acknowledged with a wave.

'How badly are you damaged?'

Tommy saw what was coming and forestalled it. Taking his megaphone, he replied: 'If you will stand by, and lend me ten good men, we'll keep her going.'

'Sure you can?'

'We're going to.'

That the men sent over from the *Wolfcub* did not relish the prospects for the next few days, was obvious. Guts Hinton set about them at once telling them that at last they were going to see something of the war. 'And don't you go being sea-sick,' he admonished them, 'there's enough mess down below as it is. Another thing; 'ave you brought your rum rations with you?'

The leading-hand in charge shook his head. 'Pity,' said Guts, 'look lively and get below!' He shepherded them down to the dark and evil-smelling interior of the submarine and shut the torpedo hatch while Bill Brown went round the upper deck to examine it for damage. One thing he found which made him look thoughtful. The towing pendant, that length of hawser secured along the upper deck from the towing slip forward, back to the after-end of the bridge, so that a towing vessel's line can be attached to it in all sorts of weather without leaving the safety of the bridge, had been completely severed by a shell-splinter; and, worse still, the actual slip, which could be operated from inside the submarine to disengage the towing pendant, was hopelessly damaged. Any towing arrangements, therefore, would have to be impoverished, and that only in the flattest of calms.

To this piece of bad news Bill thought it advisable to add the disquieting item about the continued flooding of the engine-room.

With the prospect of having to ride out a cyclone for days ahead of him, Tommy was tempted to be hanged for the whole sheep, to abandon his vessel while it was possible and to scuttle her. It depended entirely on his decision. He alone could know how badly his command was damaged. If he returned as a survivor that was all there was to it. It could be argued that, at this stage in the war, lives were more important than materials. After all, the airmen and pongos wrote off hundreds and thousands of pounds-worth of material every day. Was it worth while to bring this battered hulk into harbour?

The temptation was great. They were sorely battered, and in no real condition to face a tropical storm. Tommy felt himself slipping into the time-worn argument. Is it worth it? How did the poem go? 'We have sweethearts, we have wives; and the Lord hath spared our lives.' Was he justified in risking them further?

'Tell Mr Miles to speak to me,' he said gruffly.

In a few moments the Chief reached the bridge.

'What's all this,' said Tommy, 'about a fresh leak in the engine-room?'

'That's right,' said Mr Miles. 'I was just coming up to tell you I'd found the cause of it.'

'Ah,' said Tommy.

'Rivets,' said the Chief. 'Six of 'em. Blown clean in. I wondered where the water was comin' from.'

'What have you done?'

'Plugged 'em.'

'Anything else gone wrong?'

'No, sir,' said Mr Miles.

'Do you think the port engine will last?'

'We'll do our best, sir. Of course, we'll have to strip 'em both down when we get in. They'll need a proper refit before they're fit to do another patrol.'

'I think I can promise you that,' said Tommy, 'there's quite a lot else that'll have to be done in the electrical world.'

He took the Chief quietly into the after end of the bridge. 'Look here,' he said, 'there's a cyclone on the way. Not so funny. Are you prepared to battle through, or do you want to jump off while the going's good?'

Mr Miles gave him a puzzled look. 'You're the Skipper, sir. I'll do what I'm told,' he said.

'Come off it, Chief,' said Tommy, 'you've done magnificently so far, I want to see you live to tell the tale.'

'You wouldn't come off very well yourself, sir, if you jumped off,' said the Chief.

'To hell with that,' said Tommy, 'all I want to know is,

have you had enough, or are you game to go on?'

The Chief looked up at the lowering sky, then at the trim outline of the *Wolfcub,* then at the tired face of his Captain. It wasn't fair of Tommy to put this on to him. He was sorely tempted to say that the resources of the engine-room department were at an end; but his innate honesty forbade it. They would manage, with a bit of luck.

'I'm game, sir,' he said.

Tommy suddenly felt ready for anything. 'Good man,' he said. 'Sorry to have put it on to you like that, but you are the oldest man aboard and that counts for a good deal.'

Mr Miles put out a hand and laid it on his Captain's arm. 'I'll go anywhere with you, Tommy,' he said.

Contrary to Tommy's expectations the storm was a long time coming. There was no sudden rumble and roar of a tropical squall. It all began very prosaically. First of all a steady downpour, which flattened the sea and reduced the state of the submarine's interior to that of a dripping grotto; then the wind gradually blew up until it was fresh. Then, as if the *Gauntlet* had moved over an imaginary line into an area marked 'storm', the sea began to get really rough; and finally the weight of the wind made itself felt. It came, gust after gust, with increasing strength, and as it did so the sea, which but a few short hours before, had been a grey plain, turned into an endless series of mountain ranges, each range surmounted by peaks and crags and avalanches of white foam, and over which lay *Gauntlet*'s way to salvation.

Wolfcub soon disappeared from view; for the visibility in broad daylight was bounded by the distance it was possible to see over the tops of the waves. Occasionally *Gauntlet* would remain perched on the crest of a tumbling wave long enough for the people on her bridge to scan the surrounding sea. Then she would tip her nose down towards the purple and foam-flecked trough of the next wave, and slither swiftly to the bottom of the slope, where she would hesitate for a moment, before deciding to lift to the gradient of the next crest. Up she would come, toiling up and up, until her bows came dripping above the next summit. Then, like some great rocking horse, she would tilt slowly forward, until, once more, she tipped into the next valley.

Tommy reinforced his steering-party and changed them every half an hour; the *Gauntlet*'s men could and did manage, but those from the *Wolfcub* found the motion more than they could stomach. On the whole the *Gauntlet*, lightened of all removable ballast, was riding the waves very well, but as the strength of the gale increased there was a tendency for the wind to catch her bows as they protruded above a wave-crest, and to blow them away, so that it required full rudder and full speed on the one engine to keep her head-on to the sea.

As the light failed, the clouds, overhead, cleared for a brief moment, and showed a sky, lit by an orange coloured light which glinted like the rays reflected from the avenging angel's sword. An angry sight, terrifying in the extreme; the forces of nature putting men's puny efforts at violence to shame. Tommy had never seen such waves, even in mid-Atlantic. Each swell was twice as long as his ship and superimposed upon it were the waves generated by a severe gale. They roared and hissed and the crests blew away in spume as fast as they formed.

There would be nothing to fear from the enemy while this lasted, and there would be nothing to expect in the way of succour from any living man. As for *Wolfcub*, she was in greater danger, with her lightly built hull and superstructure, than *Gauntlet* would have been without her crippling defects. A destroyer in a full gale has to be handled so that water does not find its way down into her boiler-rooms through the vents and funnels (yes – funnels!) Tommy thought of the wounded and wondered if they had not jumped from the frying-pan into the fire. *Gauntlet*'s hull was tough and strong, as long as the patch was holding. There was no reason to worry unduly. All the same, he hoped this cyclone would move away soon, for the batteries were running down and when they died the engine would go with them.

Above all things the noise was the most scarifying. No one who has not been in a full gale can imagine the effect of this constant roaring. The *Gauntlet* had no mast, her superstructure was never more than a few yards above the surface of the sea, there were no strings or halliards upon which the wind might play a mighty tune, and yet the volume of noise transcended everything imaginable. It was deep and ominous like the sound of the biggest wind in the biggest forest of firs; it screamed with snatches of high voiced imprecations uttered by demons; it thundered incessantly with a background of dull explosions as the wave tops broke, and it hissed, hissed and hissed.

Inside the submarine speech was well-nigh impossible as the waves broke over the hull and thundered in baffled array along her superstructure and tanks. The motion amidships was tolerable; at the extreme ends unbearable. Yet it must be borne.

In the engine-room the pumping party from the *Wolfcub* pumped and vomited, vomited and pumped.

On the bridge Tommy said good-bye to the sight of those towering combers as the light went; henceforth he would hear them and often feel them, but only an occasional white cap would be visible. Now it would be impossible to warn the steering-party as he had been doing of an extra-special wave. Twelve hours of darkness lay ahead, and then what?

Tommy was standing one side of the bridge and Bill Brown the other. No one else was on deck for there was nothing to be done, no chance of sighting another vessel; if there happened to be one it was just too bad. As for *Wolfcub,* Tommy had seen enough of her Captain's seamanship not to have to worry about collision with her, she would have been taken some miles away by now to give her full freedom of action. There were, of course, mines probably adrift, and plenty of wreckage, no doubt. 'Preserve us from the dangers of the sea and the violence of the enemy.' Whoever wrote that prayer had the correct perspective.

It was impossible to talk, even in the shelter of the bridge canopy. Tommy stayed up because he felt that he should, the men below expected it. Moreover, he had a feeling that the worst of the cyclone was yet to come and when it did some quick decision might be required. The fury of the gale was such that anyone coming on the bridge from the comparative quiet of the *Gauntlet*'s interior would be stunned to a state of helplessness by the savage intensity of the wind. So it was better to remain on the alert, on the bridge.

It was necessary now to keep one's head down below the level of the canopy, if one wanted to breathe, and the eddies of wind, which struck in from each side, impinged upon the eardrums with curious effect. It was as if all the bad men who had ever been to sea, and had not returned, were stirring to a new life and cursing God as they did so, in a strange language of their own. They muttered and exclaimed, they talked and chanted in a sort of rhythmic dirge. The gates of hell were open that night, gentleness had gone, violence supreme on the face of the waters.

And now came the lightning, jagged, forked, purple, green and dazzling white, and static discharges of electricity which ran like liquid fire up the jumping wires and over the bridge. Every time the sky went light the men on the bridge were given a view of wave tops, some of them towering thirty feet above their heads, hissing and roaring in competition with the thunder-claps.

It could only be a matter of time before *Gauntlet* faltered and failed to breast such waves; and what would happen if the engine failed?

Presently Bill was relieved by Morgan Jones, who arrived to report that the barometer had dropped a quarter of an inch in less than one hour. The centre of the cyclone was clearly too close, and the speed of the *Gauntlet* too slow, for Tommy to take the action advocated in the best books to avoid remaining in the dangerous sector of the storm. It would be just a matter of sticking it.

The two men settled down to their vigil, holding on with both hands as the submarine pitched violently on the mountain-like wave tops. Down in the troughs it was possible to converse, for the waves were so high that the wind force was greatly diminished under their protective crags, but there was little to be said on such a night as this, and the constant clamour of the elements deadened the imagination and stifled thought. Nothing to do but stick it. If nothing worse than this occurred they would get through.

At the back of his mind Tommy had a picture of the movement of the submarine in relation to the waves. He felt the upward surge as she climbed to the crest, the hesitant urge as she tottered desperately in the full force of the wind, and the startlingly swift down sweep as she plunged into the valley. Then he waited for the uplift at the bottom of the trough, waited and wondered, until suddenly up she would go, up and over in a remorseless rhythm.

Presently he noticed that the rhythm was changing; the *Gauntlet* seemed to be jerking more viciously at the turning points, wave tops of fairly solid proportions were crashing into her three inch gun, and filling the bridge with broken water. Something had happened to break up the harmonic motion, the amplitude of the waves had changed and no longer suited the speed of the vessel riding to them. Tommy slowed his engine for a while but found that the steering became unmanageable. Then he speeded up and for a while all seemed well.

The *Gauntlet*'s motion was still violent, but some of the jerk had gone out of it. He decided to leave the engine speed as it was and see what would happen.

For a little longer she competed; then suddenly she seemed to get out of phase with the wave-lengths. There was a shuddering jar up forward as if she had hit something solid; her bow, instead of lifting at the bottom of the wave-trough, continued to drive downwards. To Tommy on the bridge it seemed that she had decided to dive, and he wondered momentarily if the vents had been opened and if the submarine was about to take her last plunge; then he heard Morgan Jones' voice, shrill and desperate: 'Look out, sir, it's coming!' He looked ahead and saw for a moment a towering wave crest coming from right above him, dozens of feet over the bridge and engulfed it. Solid water closed over the little structure and filled it up, plucking with mighty hands at the two men who hung on instinctively. The water was warm and softly insistent; it seemed to be persuading the men to go without a struggle. For aeons of time breathing was out of the question, then the wave passed on, and the men felt the water receding from their bodies as it drained away. Most of it went down the conning-tower hatch, making a greedy sucking sound like that of a giant bath-plug, for the engine was drawing it in instead of air. An anxious Bill at the voice-pipe asked the Captain if he was all right and stated that the flood-water was being dealt with. Tommy spat out mouthfuls of sea water.

'Are you all right, M–J?' he shouted.

'I'm O.K.,' said Morgan Jones, 'what happened?'

'She missed a step,' said Tommy, 'hope she doesn't do that too often.'

'Look out, sir,' called Morgan Jones, 'here's another one.'

Again it came upon them. Again it engulfed the bridge filling it up and flooding down into the control-room; again it half drowned the two men, but this time it did some real damage to the gun and they heard the revolving gun shield folding up like an old biscuit tin. Once again came Bill's anxious voice and once more that ghastly sucking noise as the engine made a vortex of the descending water.

'This isn't going to last,' said Tommy to himself. What should he do? Abandon the bridge? There wasn't much he could do there, except get washed over the side. If only the engine had its own source of air supply he could have shut the conning-tower hatch and kept the submarine free of water. Should he stop the engine and shut down lying stopped until the storm abated? While he thus debated his mind was made up for him. Mr Miles, braving the fury of the elements, appeared in the hatch-way.

'I'll 'ave to stop the engine, sir,' he shouted – 'thrust – ,' his voice was carried away by the wind – 'red hot!'

It only needed that, thought Tommy. He watched Mr Miles disappear and waited. Presently the vibration of the engine ceased.

'Engine stopped!' came a faint and distant voice.

'Down below, M–J!' ordered Tommy. His subordinate went quickly. Tommy waited to see what was going to happen out of sheer curiousity. The *Gauntlet* was falling away from the wind now and soon she was broadside on to the waves. Over she went on to her beam ends, and lay there as a mighty billow swept down upon her. Then, as it passed beneath her, she rose to the top of its crest and rolled violently, until, with a tremendous lurch, she skidded beam-on down the next precipitous slope. But not a drop of water came aboard. Half a dozen waves were encountered in this way and then her bows blew farther away and her stern was pointing at the oncoming seas. The after-end of her bridge, completely open, offered no protection to anyone on it. Tommy felt the mighty wind blowing in from this new direction and knew it was time to go. As he clambered into the open hatch-way and pulled the hatch to over his head, the first wave arrived crashing down upon the thin plating from the reverse direction of that which it had been designed to withstand. There wouldn't be much left of the bridge after a few hours of this sort of thing.

Down in the control-room a little knot of seamen and officers were hanging around, waiting for a verdict. Tommy looked rapidly at the patched hull and saw with relief that it seemed to be up to its work.

'Ought to have done this before,' he shouted to Bill, 'we shall be all right shut down, but – hang on!' He had felt it coming – a giant wave had picked up the *Gauntlet* and flung her on her side with such violence that men were hurled across the compartment. The Gannet had a remarkable escape; he left his own bunk, went across the whole width of the submarine and landed unhurt on a pile of blankets and hammocks which had been stowed in the gangway. Elsewhere, people were not so lucky – there were bruises and sprains and a few gashes. Down they all went on to the decks and lashed themselves stealthily while the motion continued to exceed anything that any of them had ever known.

Now, there was nothing more to be done but hang on and hope, while the *Gauntlet* lay first on one side and then on the other, whilst waves crashed over her in endless procession. And the lights got dimmer and the air began to get foul. Up on deck something big had carried away; probably the gun; they could hear it crashing round, belabouring its own bridge-work with its long barrel. The men of the submarine, and those of the *Wolfcub,* lay where they could and presently most of them dozed uneasily, worn out by the clamour of the elements and the violence of the motion.

Tommy wedged himself in his bunk and lay there in his soaking wet clothes with a turn of lashing round his body. There was something vaguely satisfactory about having one's hand forced, he felt. Now there was nothing more anyone could do. Either things got better, or – ?

Only those who have endured such conditions, and, in addition perhaps, those unfortunates who night after night have felt the agony of some mortal disease holding sleep at a distance, can understand what is really meant by a night of horror or comprehend the extraordinary ability of the human mind to hang on to hope. The motion of the submarine was such that every moment seemed bound to be her last. She did everything but roll right over, and as she did there came above the thunder of the waves those awful clanging noises which started the first horrid thoughts in the minds of those experienced seamen. The upper works were being battered flat, of that there was no doubt. What if this flattening process prevented the opening of any hatch? Quite enough to keep a man awake! But there is a limit to what any mind can take. Hours (or centuries) later Tommy fell asleep, and this was the best thing that had happened to him for many days.

CHAPTER TWENTY-THREE

'ROUNDS, sir, please.'

It was Guts, creature of routine. He had half crawled, half climbed along the gangway to the wardroom, and now stood hanging on to an overhead pipe like some giant sloth. His rotund face, with its half-halo of chins now bristled with a week's beard; his bald head was streaked with grime; his trousers had slipped so that his belly seemed to be spilling over the top of the belt that held them up in some mysterious fashion. A singlet, which once had been white, was now a dirty grey. Bill looked up at this monstrous object leering over him, and for a moment he hated the coxswain. He had just fallen off into an uneasy repose, and now he must unlash himself and risk his limbs in a tour of the submarine, because it was the time for evening rounds.

'Did I wake you, sir?' asked the coxswain with just a little too much solicitude in his voice.

Bill grunted, cast off his lashing and was precipitated out of his bunk against the evil-smelling body.

''Old up, sir,' said Guts, 'she's a bit lively tonight.'

'You're telling me,' said Bill. 'Come on!'

The motion was worse than anything either of them had ever experienced. Up on deck there were sounds, ominous sounds of metal under constant attack. The gun, now completely free to swing on its pedestal mounting, was hitting out with every motion of the vessel, first a dozen blows on one side of the bridge structure; then, as the *Gauntlet* rolled to what in any other vessel would have been over the disappearing angle, flying round to catch the other side a resounding thwack.

''Ark at that,' said the coxswain. 'I bet our lot in the *Wolfcub* are catching it. Far better 'ave left 'em – ' his voice trailed away as a violent roll dislodged him to cannon with much force against a pipe-cot.

'Turn it up, 'swain,' said the plaintive voice of Izzy Sammons. 'Can't you leave a poor bloody E.R.A. alone for a second?'

'Rounds!' retorted the coxswain.

'Struth!' said Izzy. His bright little eyes glinted in the semi-darkness. Bill grinned and passed on with a staggering rush.

'Far better 'ave left 'em aboard us,' Guts completed his sentence and tripped on a body. ''Oo's this?' he asked, as he bent down to investigate. 'Ah,' he said, with a wealth of meaning in his voice, 'as I thought. One of the Wolfcubses. What's the matter with you?' He shouted at the recumbent figure. 'Don't you feel well?'

The man's reply was unprintable.

'Rounds!' said Guts hastily. They stepped over the semi-corpse, and made the door to the torpedo-room in one rush. There, for the first time, they met a kindred spirit. The Torpedo Gunner's Mate was waiting for them, mournful as ever. He had tidied up his compartment, which was now the only one which looked like that of a normal submarine. The air was fresher there; the motion unbelievably violent. They stood hanging on with both hands and felt the surge of the waves which lifted the *Gauntlet* up and flung her down again with an infinite variety of motions.

'Pretty bad, isn't it?' shouted Bill with a grin.

Joe Parker responded with a wintry smile. 'I've known it better,' he answered. 'I hope the *Wolfcub*'s all right in this.'

'So do I,' said Bill, 'for purely selfish reasons.'

He returned to the control-room in a series of dangerous rushes. The place was dark and stank villainously of gas. A certain amount of water was dripping through the jointing of Izzy's patch, but it appeared to be holding. A few men had selected this compartment as a suitable place to doss down, but otherwise it was dead. This nerve-centre, which when submerged directed the motions of the submarine, was completely out of action.

So was the engine-room, where, in the after end, Mr Miles and two artificers were examining the plummer-blocks and thrusts.

'How is it, Chief?' shouted Bill. Mr Miles shrugged his shoulders.

'No good,' he said; he was used to talking in a din, and easily made himself heard. 'No good at all. The whole issue has dropped a tenth.'

'Any hope of getting it to go again?'

'Not till we get into 'arbour.'

'Optimist,' said Bill. He staggered to the last compartment, now completely empty, since the steering gear was not required, examined the bilges, and satisfied that all was as well as it could be he returned to the wardroom.

'Carry on, sir, please?' Guts nearly achieved a salute and fell heavily against the Captain's bunk.

'What the hell!' said Tommy, waking up. 'Take your bottom out of my bunk!'

'Beg your pardon, sir,' said Guts and turned away to his own quarters.

'Anything the matter?' shouted Tommy.

Bill shook his head. 'Rounds,' he said, 'the coxswain can't sleep unless he goes them.'

'Everything taking the strain?' asked the Captain.

'Surprisingly well,' said Bill. 'But I gather from the Chief that both engines are completely out of action. I wonder how *Wolfcub*'s getting on in this.'

Tommy yawned. 'How's the battery?' he said presently.

'Very low.' said Bill.

'Oh well,' said Tommy and turning over presently went off to sleep again.

Bill turned in and soon Mr Miles came tottering to his bunk.

The Gannet and Morgan Jones were already asleep. Bill wondered whether someone should not stay awake in order to be ready to deal with an emergency if one arose. Then he thought again and decided that there was nothing that anybody could do until the storm subsided. It was better to rest, if being thrown about in one's bunk could be so described. And so, as the fury of hell raged throughout the night, the men of the *Gauntlet* dozed uneasily and waited for the dawn.

By morning the air in the submarine was very bad. Bill had tried opening the ventilation, but so much water had come back into the trunks that at last he had been compelled to shut down as if for diving, thus, with the exception of the voice-pipe, for twelve hours the men of the *Gauntlet* had been breathing the same air. Now it was thick with carbon-dioxide, and breathing was becoming difficult. A small physical effort caused the heart to pound painfully.

Tommy lay quietly in his bunk until the hour of dawn came near. Then he clambered painfully on to the heaving deck, and staggered aft to the control-room. Bill saw him go and followed. Between them they opened up the hand-pump system for raising the periscope (the voltage was now too low to operate the hydraulic system) and roused the sleepers to work the pump. It took some considerable time to raise the heavy periscope in this manner and the pumping party was quite exhausted by the time it was up.

The motion of the submarine, just as violent as ever, made vision through the periscope almost impossible. The top window, some forty feet above the water line, was gyrating, pitching, and rolling madly, and all that Tommy managed to see was an occasional grey and white comber that leapt up to the window of the periscope as if trying to engulf it. There were many glimpses of cloud and an indeterminate horizon, but that was all. Tommy went to the barograph and tapped it more as a matter of habit than to make it sensitive, for it was getting all the vibration it needed to overcome any friction there might be in the pivots. The voice-pipe was still open, thus the barometric pressure inside the submarine kept pace with that outside of her.

He noted with satisfaction that the glass was rising, and not too steeply at that. Half-time; the storm had not been raging very long, thank God!

'What's the sea like?' asked Bill.

'Impossible to say,' said Tommy. 'Why?'

'I want to ventilate the boat,' said the First-Lieutenant, 'it's pretty fruity now.'

'All right,' said the Captain, 'open up the ventilation.'

But this turned out to be impossible, one of the shell hits had breached the ventilation trunk at water level so that it was constantly awash; solid water poured in and the valves had hastily to be shut to prevent salt water getting into the batteries.

'All right,' said Tommy. He climbed up through the lower conning-tower hatch-way, and unclipping the hatch he pushed it upwards. It rose about half an inch and then stuck and no amount of effort would lift it further. Without saying anything he descended, and climbed into the gun access-trunk, where he unclipped both hatches and tried to open them. They too, would not budge. Whatever had happened on deck had effectively prevented the movement of these hatches. Unless they could be levered open, life was going to be a parlous matter. There were four other hatches, but they could only be opened in harbour, or in flat calms. 'Nasty sensation,' thought Tommy, 'entombed – as the papers like to describe it.' He went to the wardroom and shook Mr Miles. As quietly as possible he imparted the dread information. Mr Miles clambered out of his bunk, staggered forward, pulled Izzy out of his bunk, and together the pair of them went down aft to the engine-room whence, presently, they re-emerged armed with pinch bars and screw jacks.

'Soon 'ave it open,' said Izzy and for a moment Tommy believed him.

After half an hour's work, however, they only succeeded in pushing one hatch up six inches. From what they could see, said the Chief, the whole of the top fabric of the bridge had been beaten flat by the action of the waves, assisted by the gun. The chances of pushing the hatches up far enough to get out of them were not good.

On the other hand, a certain amount of fresh air could be drawn in by working a blower motor (as long as the current lasted) and when the sea subsided it would be possible to get out through one of the hatches in the hull. It was serious only if the enemy sent out fresh search parties. From now on the *Gauntlet* was almost completely helpless, or, as the Staff-Officer would have put it, 'non-operational'.

CHAPTER TWENTY-FOUR

ALL that day the gale raged and the plight of the men, locked inside the darkened submarine became worse. Although they knew that when the sea subsided they would be able to get out, and although, by taking turns at the crack of the conning-tower hatch, they were able to get some fresh air into their lungs, they all felt themselves to be trapped, for, in a sudden emergency they would not be able to help themselves.

Towards nightfall they became aware of a lessening of the motion and Tommy informed them that the wind was no longer at hurricane force. They took counsel amongst themselves and presently Bert Toogood made so bold as to suggest a remedy to their present situation to Bill Brown.

'You see, sir,' he was saying, 'if you was to trim the stern up as high as possible, you could open the after escape hatch long enough to get a working party on deck.'

Bill considered the project carefully.

'Not much fun for the working party,' he said, 'the seas are breaking over the conning-tower by the sound of it.'

'The working party,' said Toogood, 'would have to lash themselves on. Then, if one of them went into the oggin somebody else could pull him out.'

'How would you get from the after escape-hatch on to the bridge?' asked Bill.

'I've thought of that,' said Toogood. 'The second coxswain has got some slip-hooks. As soon as a man gets out on deck, he's wearing a life-line all ready, and he clips himself on to the jumping wire. That'll keep him aboard.'

'H'm,' said Bill, 'how many men would be in the working party?'

'Not more than four, sir.'

'Who?'

'Me and three others,' said Toogood.

'One of you will have to stand out,' said Bill. 'I shall go in charge – if the Skipper agrees to the plan. I'll go and talk to him.'

Tommy listened to Bill's suggestion; he was just as anxious to open the hatches as anyone, and he saw the wisdom of getting it done as soon as possible, but he doubted whether any man could live for long in that jumble up top. After a while of thought he had an idea.

'Tell you what,' he said, 'blow some oil out of one of the fuel tanks and we'll see what effect it has on the waves.'

Away sped Bill to try the experiment, which was entirely successful. Soon a brownish film could be seen through the periscope to have spread around the *Gauntlet* and the noise of breaking waves was considerably diminished.

'Why didn't I think of that before?' said Tommy. 'All right, Number One, we'll have a bang at it. Who are your party?'

'It was Toogood's idea,' said Bill.

Tommy shook his head. 'I don't want to lose my Petty Officer Telegraphist,' he said, 'he's too valuable. As soon as that hatch is open and he can rig another aerial I want him to go on listening in for *Wolfcub.*'

'He'll be very disappointed,' said Bill. 'I proposed to go in charge.'

Tommy looked at him for a moment. 'I see,' he said. 'Let's have a word with Toogood.'

When the Petty Officer Telegraphist had reported, Tommy said: 'I'm afraid you can't go for two reasons. Firstly, I can't spare you; secondly, I want men who are accustomed to working with tools. It'll be a case of hammer and chisel stuff.'

'Very good, sir,' said Bert.

'The First-Lieutenant will go in charge,' said Tommy.

Toogood looked reproachfully at the man who had betrayed him. 'Very good, sir,' he said.

'Right,' said Tommy. 'I'll not forget that you volunteered – twice for the most hazardous jobs.'

'Thank you, sir,' said Toogood and went away.

'Now, Chief,' said Tommy to Mr Miles, 'I want three lusty volunteers, used to working with their hands.'

'Aye, aye,' said the Chief, 'I'll go and tell them off.' He went away and came back in a few minutes.

'Chief E.R.A. Sammons and Stoker Macnalty have volunteered,' he said.

'Who's the third?' asked Tommy.

Mr Miles looked at him. 'I'm pretty good with a chisel and 'ack-saw,' he said.

'Two officers,' said Tommy.

'And two ratings,' Bill reminded him.

'I suppose so. All right. The sooner the better. Flood all forward auxiliaries.'

The news of the project spread like wildfire. A ripple of excitement went through the boat and there was much eager anxiety to be up and doing. Presently the bows of the *Gauntlet* began to tilt downwards and the stern to rise as the shifting of ballast took effect. When the maximum angle had been achieved the volunteer party, wearing life-lines and carrying tools strapped to their bodies, gathered under the after escape-hatch, accompanied by Tommy and a party of hands.

'First,' said Tommy, 'we'll see what it's like up top.'

He unscrewed the clips and gingerly raised the hatch an inch or so. An immediate gout of water flooded down momentarily, then ceased, and then came again as the waves alternately washed over, and receded from the stern.

It would be a bit risky to throw the hatch wide open, and, if anything jammed it, it would be fatal. Tommy turned to the working party and gave his orders.

'You've got to move like scalded cats,' he said. 'A lot of water's going to come in and I can't give you more than thirty seconds for the lot of you. First one out pulls the next one up. Savvy?'

They nodded.

'You first,' said Tommy to Bill. 'Good luck.'

Bill climbed the little ladder, followed closely by the Chief, while the other two stood ready to follow.

'All right!' said Tommy, 'carry on!'

There was a crash as the hatch flew open, daylight suddenly lit the dark interior. Tommy saw the haggard faces around him for a moment and then the water came in, green and solid. It was overpowering in its quantity and seemed as if it would never stop. Then, suddenly as it began, it stopped and the four men scurried up the ladder. As a second wave arrived the hatch was slammed down and clipped and the hand-pump was started on the water which had come in.

Tommy made his way thoughtfully back to the control-room, and waited for the sound of men working overhead.

For a very long time, nothing happened. Then he heard the noise of hammering, and felt great relief. He had been so afraid that that wave had carried them all away. Rapidly climbing the conning-tower he pushed up the hatch to its limit, and shouted to the men on top.

'Are you all right?' he asked.

The hammering ceased for a moment and a footstep sounded close overhead. 'It's me, sir,' said the Chief. 'Macnalty went over the side, and Number One went after 'im. I saw 'im get to young Mac, and then I never saw them again. Both gone,' he added.

Tommy had never felt worse in his life. 'Do you want any more help?' he asked.

'Me and Izzy will manage,' said the Chief. 'Cor! you ought to see what's 'appened 'ere.'

The hammering was resumed and Tommy went down, sick at heart to break the news to the crew. Bill Brown; the finest of the fine. It was difficult to believe. Anyone but him. The burden was getting intolerable.

They crouched about, waiting for the rescue party to cut away the plating which hampered the opening of the hatch, and there was little enough conversation. It was still difficult to imagine the *Gauntlet* without her First-Lieutenant. Even coxswain was speechless for a while and when some time later an oval of light showed that the conning-tower hatch was now open there was little jubilation. Macnalty was well-liked too, but most of the feeling was that he shouldn't have gone over the side.

'What'd he want to do that for,' said Guts – 'course Jimmy 'ad to go after 'im.'

Tommy climbed up the ladder and viewed the scene of desolation on the bridge with sombre eyes. Then he pulled himself together and thanked the two survivors for their stalwart work. Mr Miles was plainly distressed.

'I reckon it was the oil-fuel on the water what got 'im,' he said. 'One moment we saw him, didn't we, Izzy, and the next, he was gone. 'Straordinary.'

Tommy was not satisfied. He climbed up on the standard and searched the tumbling waters with all his might. Bill Brown was a good swimmer, but, of course a shark might have got him.

The *Gauntlet* was lying stern to the sea, so Tommy searched chiefly ahead in line with her bows. It was getting dark now, soon it would be black as pitch and that would be the end of all hope. With his arms locked round the big periscope he searched and searched. Something told him that the men were still afloat. The trouble was that the waves were still so big that he couldn't see over them. Unless he happened to be looking at the right moment there wasn't a hope of seeing a man in the water.

Down below, Morgan Jones, stepping manfully into the shoes of his predecessor, blew the forward tanks and restored the *Gauntlet* to her normal trim. The gloom, both physical and mental was completely unrelieved. Then, suddenly, down the voice-pipe, came the excited voice of the Captain, calling for Mr Miles, who had gone below exhausted.

The Chief came running in to the control-room, naked, save for a small singlet. 'Yes, sir?' he called.

'Can you get an engine to go?' asked Tommy. 'I think I've seen them right ahead.'

The Chief shook his head at the voice-pipe. 'The bearing's all gone,' he said.

'A couple of minutes will do,' said Tommy, 'just to get closer to them.'

'It'll put paid to 'em,' said the Chief.

'Never mind that,' said Tommy. His voice faded as he turned to have another look at the objects in the water. 'It's them all right,' he said presently, 'let me know when you're ready to go ahead!'

Now the excitement was intense. The two men were not gone; once again the wardroom Flunkey climbed to the wreck of the bridge, ready to help in the rescue work, while the Chief and his minions primed the port fuel-rail, and wondered what would happen when the engine began to fire.

'Port engine ready, sir,' said a voice from below.

Tommy swung the telegraph to 'Half-ahead', and gave orders to the steersman, who had taken up their stations in the after compartment.

There was a rumble, and a rattle, some muffled explosions, and the whole vessel began to shake as if it was being driven over cobble-stones.

'There they are, sir,' called the signalman, pointing a frenzied finger right ahead of them. 'Only two waves away now!'

Tommy made a dart at the telegraph but the engine stopped with a dull disintegrating sort of noise which told its story only too plainly. 'Never mind,' said Tommy.

'Shall I go, sir?' said the Flunkey. He had a line round his body.

Now the swimmers were only fifty yards away but it was obvious that they couldn't do more than keep themselves afloat. Bill Brown was supporting the Stoker, who appeared to be unconscious.

Tommy began to imagine that he could see sharks' fins in all directions. The *Gauntlet* was losing way now.

'Go on,' said Tommy.

The Flunkey dived in. His swimming was magnificent, and he reached the exhausted men just in time. Casting off his line he tied it round the pair of them.

'Haul away!' ordered Tommy. The men on the bridge, slithering and slipping on the shattered plates, pulled the men alongside and then, regardless of the danger they themselves were in, went down and man-handled them up on to the top of the conning-tower. It was a magnificent piece of team work. They all worked like maniacs, delighted to have their messmates back from the dead.

Bill was barely conscious; he had been supporting the other man since he had gone in after him, for Macnalty's head was hurt when he went overboard and he could do nothing for himself. They took them both below, and turned them in, while the tropical night closed in upon them and the rough seas slowly subsided.

CHAPTER TWENTY-FIVE

By dawn on the next day two things had happened. Firstly, the sea wind had dropped away, leaving a steep swell which was rapidly decreasing. Secondly, the electric batteries were now so weak that the lamp filaments only glowed with a feeble glimmer. In spite of the conditions aboard, however, everybody had had some rest, though from now on there would be no hot food or drink.

Within two hours of daylight *Wolfcub* appeared as if by magic. The Captain of that ship again demonstrated that he was no slouch at seamanship. His method of finding the *Gauntlet* was to go to the position where he'd last seen her and then to steam down wind along the track on which she would have drifted.

'How are you?' shouted the loud hailer.

'Glad to see you,' shouted Tommy. 'My batteries are dead and both engines seized up, and my bridge is flat but otherwise I'm fine, thank you.'

'I'll take you in tow.'

'Thanks.'

'Do you still want my sailors?'

Tommy looked at the leading hand of the *Wolfcub*'s party, and saw the anxiety on the man's face. They had not enjoyed their sojourn in *Gauntlet*; that was clear. Now that the bilges were practically dry the fewer men he had on board the better.

'No thanks,' he replied.

The man's face was a study.

'I'll send over for them.'

'Do, and send a fanny full of hot tea while you're about it – we haven't had a cup o' char for days.'

'O.K.'

The whaler came over and Tommy had a talk with the officer in charge. All the *Gauntlet*'s wounded had stuck the cyclone extraordinarily well, as had the *Wolfcub* herself and they were feeling pretty pleased with themselves aboard her. To have ridden out a full-bodied cyclone is a good experience to have behind one.

'You must have had a sticky time, sir,' said the officer.

'Yes,' said Tommy. 'I thought at one time you'd have to use a tin-opener to get us out. Tell your Skipper that my towing arrangements are shot to pieces. We'll take your line and secure it to the foremost bollards. Tell him not to pay out too much at a time or my people won't be able to hold the weight of it.'

The whaler went away crowded with men, who showed quite clearly how relieved they were to be leaving. As soon as it was alongside the *Wolfcub* had hoisted in, the Captain of the destroyer manoeuvred his ship within the proverbial biscuit's toss, a heaving line was thrown across and the *Gauntlet*'s crew pulled the heavy towing wire aboard. When it was fast the *Wolfcub* went slowly ahead and took the strain. There was a barely perceptible jerk and the *Gauntlet* began once more to move ahead through the water. Gradually the destroyer worked up speed until she was doing nearly nine knots.

'At this rate,' said Bill, 'we shall be there in forty-eight hours.'

Bill had quite recovered from his narrow escape, though he was a little more thoughtful when he spoke. Macnalty, apart from a severe headache, was fairly well and steadfastly refused to be put aboard the destroyer. So did some of the technical staff of the submarine. Tommy had had the idea of getting rid of as many men as possible into the *Wolfcub*, but this was a most unpopular move. Izzy Sammons, himself, had the effontery to speak to his Captain.

'If it's all the same to you, sir,' he said, 'we'd like to see this thing out. It may be our last trip together.'

'It will be,' said Tommy gruffly, 'all right, Sammons, have it your own way.'

'Thank you, sir,' said Izzy and went away to tell the news.

'I went up to the Skipper and I said: "Now look 'ere, we started in this racket and we're going to flaming well see it out to the bitter end," ' was his description of the interview.

'Blasted cheek,' said Guts, 'trouble with you Tiffies is that you don't know your place. Poor old Tommy,' he added.

'What'll 'appen to him?' asked Izzy.

'If he had 'is deserts, he'd get a perishing V.C., or some-such,' said Guts, 'as it is though this lot'll take a bit of laughing off. Fact is, he never ought to 'ave surfaced.'

'What do *you* know about it?' Izzy sprang to the aid of his beloved Tommy.

'I know what I'm saying, you mark my words. Old Sanderson won't like it a little bit.'

'Can't we do something?'

'What? Put in a request to the *Captain S/M* and say: "Don't be too 'ard on our Tommy – 'e's done 'is best?" ' The Coxswain spat into a bucket.

'Look,' said Izzy, 'if 'e 'adn't taken on that ship, *Goose* would never 'ave torpedoed that destroyer. See?'

'And you wouldn't be chawing your fat 'ere. Two blacks don't make a white. Any fool knows that.'

'If they lay a finger on 'im I'll – I'll – '

'What'll you do?' interrupted Guts.

'Write to me Member of Parliament.'

'Fat lot of good that'll do,' said the Coxswain. 'All the same I'd like to see Sanderson's face when 'e sees our defect list. The only thing that isn't spitchered is my rum measure.'

'Not surprising as you never use it,' said Izzy. 'Look 'ere, 'swain, there 'ave been times when I 'aven't loved you like a brother, but you and me are agreed about Tommy. Can't we so something about it? I mean, 'ow is the old man to know what sort of show 'e's put up in the past how-many-is-it days?'

'Tommy'll put it on paper,' said the Coxswain.

'Can you see 'im blowin' 'is own trumpet?' said Izzy, ' 'e's too blasted modest.'

'I see what you mean,' said Guts. 'I'll 'ave to look it up in the Regulations.'

'What will you look up?' asked Izzy.

'Look,' said Guts, 'there's always a way round if you use the Regulations, or the Articles of War, or both, proper. What you do is find something you aren't allowed to do and then you put in a request to ask *Captain S/M* for permission to do it.'

'I don't see.'

'Thick 'eaded, that's you,' said Guts, 'listen. Supposing it's against the regulations to give the Skipper a parting present, and I fancy it is. Well then, I put in my request and see the *Captain S/M*.'

' "Why do you want to give your Commanding Officer a

gift, my good fellow," he says.'

'Like hell he does,' murmured Izzy.

' "Because, sir," I reply, " 'e did so very well and saved all our blasted lives, and we don't want 'im to forget us." See?'

'With nobs on,' said Izzy, 'that's not a bad idea of yours, 'swain.'

'Ah,' said Guts, 'you can always find it in the regulations. Did I ever tell you 'ow I got a new set of teeth down to 'is Majesty?'

' 'Undreds of times,' said Izzy. 'What made you join the Navy; man o' your wit'd go a long way in business.'

'D'you think so?' Guts was disarmed by the compliment.

'A very long way,' said Izzy getting up – 'as far as Dartmoor, I reckon, or farther.'

He moved away into the darkness before Guts could think of anything more to say.

The object of the two men's conversation was also thinking of the future. By the aid of a hand torch he was scribbling notes from the control-room log-book, in preparation for the writing of his patrol report, when he got into harbour. However he looked at it it was a proper mess-up. The only thing to do was to write a full and detailed report of everything that had taken place, without expressing any opinion of the wisdom of the action he had taken. Furthermore, he must put in a list of recommendations for promotion or decoration. Everybody had behaved so well that it would be a very long list. Then, of course, there would be the relations of the two dead men, and after that – Audrey.

Presently the Signalman came down with a long message from *Capentaria*. '*Gauntlet from S/M (N)*,' it ran. '*A preliminary report of proceedings is to be signalled forthwith.*'

Tommy whistled to himself.

'He's asked for it and he shall have it,' he said and thereupon he settled down to work. The report went up to the bridge, a page at a time and was signalled to *Wolfcub*, who would then code it and transmit to *Carpentaria*.

CHAPTER TWENTY-SIX

Two days later the *Wolfcub*, with *Gauntlet* in tow, steamed through the gate in the boom defence and came to a halt in the protected waters of the harbour. It was raining hard, the same sizzling downpour that had fallen upon the *Gauntlet* when she had so frantically prepared for sea. The Skipper of the tug who came alongside said that it had been raining ever since and would probably go on for ever more, for all he cared.

'Can't keep a thing dry,' he said, 'what 'ave you been up to?'

Tommy grinned weakly. 'It's too long a story. You'll hear about it later,' ('in the courts-martial returns,' he nearly added). Then, remembering his manners, he made a grateful signal to the *Wolfcub* acknowledging his debt to the destroyer who had pulled them into safety.

With the exception of the steering party aft, the whole of the remaining crew was gathered on deck; looking at the sad little scene as if it was a sunny day at Blackpool. They cracked jokes and showed their evident relief at the prospect of getting out of the dark and evil smelling *Gauntlet* into a fresh-water bath, a shave and some clean clothes; and then, who knows? a whole bottle of cold beer.

It was all something of an anti-climax, their arrival alongside. It coincided with the dinner hour. This, together with the constant and heavy rain, brought nobody on deck, save the spare crew, who took the *Gauntlet*'s lines and secured them, scuttling away to their roast beef and Yorkshire pudding, just as soon as they could. If they noticed the battle-and-storm-scarred appearance of the *Gauntlet*, they showed little or no surprise. As for the officers they were not present in large numbers, though the Duty Officer could be seen sheltering in the wardroom lobby.

A most discouraging reception, thought Tommy; evidently his preliminary report had not cut very much ice. He looked across at the trim submarine to which *Gauntlet* was secured, and then at his own battered hulk. In the past week there had been a number of occasions when he had not expected to see the *Carpentaria* again. Now it appeared that those aboard her couldn't care less. He felt immensely tired and conscious of his dishevelled appearance. He could not, he felt, go and report to Captain Sanderson in this filthy state; if he did he would probably be told to clean himself up.

Things had gone wrong on the fo'c'sle; Bill Brown was angry about something. 'Hi!' he shouted at the retreating figures of the spare crew, 'get me a spare gang-plank.'

The Leading Seaman in charge returned. ' 'Aven't you got a gang-plank, sir?' he asked.

'No,' said Bill.

The man scratched his head. 'I don't thing there is a spare one, sir.'

'Not a spare one,' said Bill with heavy irony. 'Then we shall have to stay on board here for ever.'

'Flaming fine lot of muckers,' said Guts (or words to that effect), 'anybody'd think we'd been out on a day's running instead of facin' 'orrible death in henemy waters. 'Ere you, 'Uggins, nip down into the Chippy's shop and you'll find plenty of timber. And look alive, d'you hear.' The man trotted off obediently, rounding up his party as he did so.

'Cor,' said Guts, 'they just don't know there's a war on. That's the long and short of it.'

Tommy half heard the contretemps, but was too tired to care whether there was a plank or not. He'd been doing much, both physically and mentally, and now that the cloak of his immediate responsibility had dropped from him, he felt completely finished. If there was no gang-plank he would sit where he was until there was one. Anyway, no one seemed to care aboard the depot-ship. It was as if they were deliberately cold-shouldering him.

When, however, at long last, the men arrived with a plank, it became apparent that this odd reception was the result of an accident.

Commander Wardle himself risked life and limb to come tottering over the gang-way to greet Tommy.

'My dear chap,' he panted, 'that half-witted officer of the day mistook you for another boat which has been docking. What did you think of us? I'd have cleared the lower deck and given you a chuck up.'

('Sh'd think so') whispered Guts.

'The Captain's ashore at a conference until tomorrow,' went on Wardle, 'so you can get into a bath right away. I'm sending the technical staff out to take over completely so that your chaps can clean up and rest; and, by the way,' he added, 'there's some beer been kept for you from the last ration.'

'Thank you, sir,' said Tommy.

'You must be tired,' said the Commander.

Tommy looked at him and pondered for a moment. 'I suppose I must,' he said, 'but there are one or two things to do. I must have a charge on my batteries at once.'

'That's all right, sir,' said Bill, 'I'll look after that.'

'I shall need a portable pump,' went on Tommy, 'she's making a bit of water and all my electrics are out of – '

'That's all right, sir,' said Mr Miles, 'I'll fix it all up.'

'Then I must go and see the Captain,' said Tommy.

'I said he was ashore,' said Commander Wardle.

'So you did,' said Tommy, 'so you did.'

'Well,' said the Commander, after a pause, 'no point in standing in the rain. See you later.' He swayed back over the springing planks and Tommy followed. As he stepped off his ship the Coxswain, without orders, produced a Bosun's Call and piped him over the side. It was a gesture that the ship's company fully understood. They wanted Tommy to know what they thought of him.

Bill Brown watched the small untidy figure walking to the ship across the other submarines and something suspiciously near to tears came to his eyes. 'Bloody nearly "out" on his feet,' he said, 'what a performance!'

The upper deck of the *Carpentaria* rocked most disconcertingly as Tommy made his way aft to the smoking-room. It would be a couple of days before this lack of balance was overcome. Tommy turned in at the open door and made straight for the letter rack. A small packet of mail awaited him. He sorted through them savagely and did not find the one he hoped for. Audrey had not written. He wondered what that meant. A few officers, resting after their midday meal, looked drowsily up at the unkempt figure and were too sleepy to make any remark which was worth making. Tommy went out and down the after hatch to his cabin. He couldn't remember the number of it for certain but when he pulled a curtain aside and saw a photograph of Audrey he reckoned he was home. He sat down on the wicker chair and picked up the photo to feast his eyes upon somebody whom he had not expected to see again. His mind was blank, save for the clear recognition that his wife's portrait was in his hands.

He sat looking at it. There were footsteps in the lobby outside and then the curtain of the cabin was pulled back. Someone gave an ejaculation of horror and Tommy turned to see what was the matter.

The Staff-Officer, Twiggs, was staring at him with a look of fear in his eyes which slowly faded as one of recognition replaced it.

'What's the matter?' asked Tommy.

'Oh, hullo,' said Twiggs.

'What were you staring at me like that for?' demanded Tommy.

'I'm sorry. I wasn't expecting to see anybody here.'

'Why not? It's my cabin isn't it?'

'No,' said Twiggs, 'it *was* George Carter's. Seeing you there gave me an awful shock. I thought he'd come back from the dead.'

'No,' said Tommy, '*he* hasn't.' He got up and took a hold on himself. 'I'm so damn' stupid,' he said, 'that I mistook the cabin.'

'You must be tired.'

'It wasn't that,' said Tommy, 'it was the photo. By the way, why hasn't it been packed up? George Carter was lost two weeks ago.'

'His sister in the Wrens is coming out and said she would attend to his gear – '

'Coming out?'

'Yes. I understand so.'

'When?'

'I don't know.'

'Don't you know anything?'

Twiggs was annoyed. 'There's no need to talk to me like that, Woodstock. Even if you are tired. Anyway, what's it got to do with you?'

'I am married to her,' said Tommy. He took the photograph and found his way to his own cabin. Laying it down he went back to Twiggs.

'I didn't know,' said Twiggs.

'No reason why you should,' said Tommy, 'sorry I bit you.'

'Oh, that's all right. Every submarine captain does that first thing when he gets in from patrol. I'm used to it.'

'I suppose you must be.' (Audrey!)

'It isn't my fault that I have to be chair-borne. It's my blasted eye-sight.'

'I know,' said Tommy, 'damn' bad luck.'

'Chaps seem to think that because they have all the fun and excitement in the war they can come back when they're tired and pitch in to the poor bloody S.O. (O.).'

'Oh, quite,' said Tommy, 'I'll remember that in future.'

'You won't,' said Twiggs, 'but no offence taken. Anybody can see your nerves are all to pieces. You must have had one hell of a time.'

'I did, but they aren't.'

'What caused it all?'

Tommy yawned. 'You'll have to wait for my report,' he said.

'Ah,' said the Staff-Officer, 'I was going to ask. Will it be ready today?'

'If my Sub doesn't fall asleep over the typewriter it will,' said Tommy. 'He and I scribbled it out by the light of a pocket torch, in order to have something ready for you.'

'Good,' said Twiggs, 'I always like to run through it before *Captain S/M* gets it – I'm usually able to clear up any ambiguities.'

'Quite right,' said Tommy. Suddenly the thought that Audrey, his Audrey, was coming rapidly towards him, penetrated to his inner mind. It was too good to be true. 'You are sure that – she – is coming out?' he asked.

Twiggs looked offended again. 'I said so once,' he began.

'Sorry, sorry,' said Tommy, 'just over-anxiety, that's all.' After all, what did anything matter if he was to see his wife again? She would understand when he told her he'd mucked everything, nearly lost his ship and put paid to two of his best men. What did it matter if this pompous ass of a Staff-Officer kept taking umbrage, what would it matter if Captain Sanderson chucked him out, what would it matter if he never saw his crew again? No, that would matter, but not in the same way. Audrey!

'What did you say?' He'd forgotten the Staff-Officer was still there.

'I said sorry,' said Tommy, 'and I meant it. Now run along like a dear good chap and let me have a bath.' The Staff-Officer turned to go and a new idea struck Tommy.

'By the way,' he said, 'what were you going to do in Carter's cabin?'

A deep blush spread over Twiggs' face. He tried to say something and failed.

Tommy laughed softly. 'She is beautiful, isn't she?' he said. 'Don't apologise. A cat may look at a Queen.'

Twiggs bolted with all the appearance of a man caught in a shameful act. Tommy went to his bath chuckling.

If the reader has so far been shown the *Carpentaria* through the eyes of tired and disappointed 'submariners' he should not be misled into thinking that depot-ship staffs are incompetent and callous camp-followers. That is only how they appear to the unthinking men whose whole beings are subject to a violent reaction at the end of a long period of strain. If there is such a place as heaven it is more than likely that the angels in charge of the reception committee catch it equally hot from those mortals who, at last, have come safe to that celestial depot-ship.

Bill Brown, as ever, changed the least. He went on as usual, but even his manner was a shade more impatient when dealing with the depot-ship staff. On this occasion, however, there was nothing at which to cavil. An army of men had come aboard, and had set to work mending everything which was not beyond repair. Already two giant black snake-like cables had been passed across to the *Gauntlet* and fed down the conning-tower hatch to the switch-board. The batteries were getting a transfusion which would save their lives. Already the interior of the submarine was lit from end to end by filaments which glowed brilliantly.

A stream of chattering sailors, carrying mess kit, and dirty clothes was wending its way across the planks, back to the *Gauntlet*'s crew's mess-deck in the fore-part of the *Carpentaria*.

Guts was on deck rebuking everybody and everything.

'That's right,' he said as he caught sight of Izzy Sammons, 'rats deserting the sinking ship as usual. What about your engines, aren't you going to mend 'em?'

'Turn it up,' said Izzy disdainfully.

'Well, what's the hurry? I got a couple o' gash noggins

down below. Could you go one?'

Izzy was tempted. 'Very 'andsome, I'm sure. I'll be back as soon as I've read me mail. I'm a married man, you know.'

'I might o' guessed you were,' said Guts. 'What do you want?' He turned ferociously on a young supply assistant who wilted before the demeanour of this man with a face like a giant gooseberry.

'The Chief says he'll open the slop store for the *Gauntlet*'s crew for half an hour after stand-easy,' he said. He moved quickly away but not fast enough.

'Did he now,' the Coxswain began gently enough. 'What's your name, little man?'

'Macdonald,' said the inoffensive messenger.

'And what's the Chief's name?' went on the Coxswain, with a deceptively silky turn to his speech.

'Parkinson,' said the messenger.

'Well, Mr Macdonald,' said the Coxswain impressively, 'you will kindly convey my compliments to Chief Supply Petty Officer Parkinson (God rot his soul), and tell 'im that when I want his store open I'll let 'im know. What does he think we are? Ordinary seamen on a training-class cruise? You tell 'im to come down 'ere and take a butcher's at what we've bin puttin' up with – and don't stand there in the gangway blockin' everybody's exit. Some people want to get their 'eads down and what's more' – he followed the discomfited messenger with ever-increasing violence in his voice – 'some people don't know THERE'S A WAR ON!'

Morgan Jones, arriving on deck at that moment, put on his most professional manner. 'We'll have to watch our blood pressure, Hinton,' he said.

'Oh 'ullo, sir,' said the Coxswain with forced geniality.

Morgan Jones stopped and thought for a moment. Then he said quietly: 'We did a good job with the wounded, Coxswain. They're all getting better.'

Guts looked uncertain as to what line to take.

'They owe it largely to you,' said Morgan Jones.

'Oh, no, sir,' said the Coxswain. He too could be handsome.

'No,' said Morgan Jones, 'if you hadn't been so bloody unco-operative to start with I wouldn't have had the guts to go through with it.'

'I don't know what you mean, sir.'

'Don't you?' said Morgan Jones and passed on. He was followed by the Gannet, carrying a portable typewriter and a sheaf of papers. Even Guts's heart was melted by this gallant young officer. He showed his affection by biting the wardroom Flunkey. 'Lettin' an officer carry 'is own gear,' he said, 'what do you think this is, the Red Navy?'

'Turn it up, 'swain,' said the man who had practised life-saving at sea. 'See what I got?' He showed the bottle of gin.

''Ere,' said the Coxswain, 'you can't take that aboard without it goin' through the gangway wine and spirit book. You know that.'

'First-Lieutenant's orders,' said the Flunkey, 'and it is going through the gangway book, so don't jump to conclusions.'

'Just because you can swim,' said the Cox'n. 'Anyway, I never 'ad any use for gin – woman's drink.'

Bert Toogood followed, walking delicately. For a man who had endured so much he looked well and at peace with the world.

''Ullo, Bert,' said the Coxswain. 'Proper turn out, wasn't it? Reckon you did as much as any to get us 'ome – could you go one?'

'After I've seen me mail,' said Bert as he tiptoed on his way.

'What's the matter with all you blokes,' demanded the Coxswain, 'afraid your wives 'ave left you, or what? Yes, Joe?'

The Torpedo Gunner's Mate was sponging his fingers with cotton waste as he said: 'Them six fish ought to come back out o' them tubes. I 'aven't 'ad 'em out for a week.'

'Tomorrow, old man,' said Guts. 'Tomorrow. Jimmy-the-One said we was to Pipe Down. Now, what about 'arf a gill?'

'If you say so,' said the mournful Parker. 'Come to think of it I do feel a bit low.'

'At last!' said the Coxswain, 'I thought everybody 'ad lost their natural h'appetites.'

As they went below Mr Miles limped past.

'I knew this would 'appen,' he complained. 'It's getting wet feet as does it.'

CHAPTER TWENTY-SEVEN

It is traditional among submarine officers that the first night in harbour after a patrol should be spent wassailing. However tired a man may be he will not immediately be able to relax. Hence this custom, founded, as ever, on human necessity. Commander Wardle, who knew the form, always kept a little wine-stock up his sleeve for the sailors home from the sea, and only a very little was needed to bowl over men who had not touched more than an occasional noggin since that last memorable gin-party. They appeared, scrubbed pink from the unaccustomed bath, they smoked vigorously and each with a glass in his hand, gave his opposite numbers, from the submarines alongside, some inkling of what had been going on. They made jokes of most of the events and passed over the sadnesses by common consent. They talked before dinner, and at dinner, and would have talked after dinner if old Wardle hadn't sat down at the piano and banged out some bawdy tunes. The mess joined in with a will, and for a brief hour or so, those tired young men forgot the past, and neglected the future. With eyes which threatened to close at any moment they grouped themselves round the piano and got themselves really exhausted, so that they were past being able to go to bed. When the wardroom bar had been locked, and Wardle had closed the piano, they walked about on deck still talking, and, after that, gathered in knots in some cabin or other. It was as if they dreaded the solitude of their bunks. Even so, midnight saw them turned in, to fall into heavy, but short-lived sleep, from which their tortured nerves would bring them to sudden wakefulness, at some chance sound, or even at some more profound silence. It would not be possible for several days for anyone to turn in quietly with a book, and to drop off for eight hours' uninterrupted slumber. Man is an adaptable animal, but even a 'submariner' needs time to get used to the cessation of strain.

In the morning they awoke more dead than alive, and the condition of the ship's company was no better. Now, the period of the great let-down had begun, a feeling of intense depression pervaded. The thing that had kept them going was missing and the future loomed ahead bleak but uncertain.

There would, of course, be a period in a rest-camp after the necessary work had been done, and the *Gauntlet* put into dock, but after that some change was bound to take place, and seamen abominate change.

Tommy, who had drunk practically nothing the night before, felt as if he had consumed the entire contents of Watney's Brewery. Even the thought of Audrey's proximity did not sustain him for the forthcoming ordeal.

The report, duly typed and signed in triplicate, had gone into the Staff-Officer and an appointment with *Captain S/M* fixed after his return aboard and after he had read the report. Now it was necessary to wait for the moment. Tommy's acquaintance with Captain Sanderson had been but brief, and he had not got on to terms with him. He had no idea what attitude the Captain would adopt, and the Staff-Officer was not likely to be helpful. Already he had pointed out various errors and omissions in the report.

'You haven't stated,' he said, as he turned over the pages, 'what type of aircraft the enemy was employing. That's very useful information, you know.'

'Yes, I know,' said Tommy, 'we were rather too busy to make notes.'

'And the ship that you engaged,' went on Twiggs, 'would she have been the *Akurai,* converted from the Singapore-Java ferry service?'

'I couldn't say,' said Tommy.

'Pity,' said Twiggs. And so on.

It was with a dryness of the mouth and beating of the heart that Tommy went to his interview, and as he knocked on the Captain's door he felt like a schoolboy going up for six of the best.

'Come in.' Captain Sanderson had the report in front of him. He had made some notes and had written quite a lot on a separate piece of paper.

He got up as Tommy entered, and looked keenly at him.

'I expect you want to know what I think of it all,' he said. 'This is what I propose to say:

'The story of the return of H. M. S. *Gauntlet is an epic in the history of the Submarine Service. I consider that Lieutenant Woodstock displayed courage, endurance and leadership of the highest order and his efforts received magnificent support from his Officers and Ship's Company, who never lost heart and responded to every call made upon them.'*

When he had finished Tommy felt that he should say something. A dry little 'Thank you' was all he could manage.

'And now,' said his Captain, 'that you know what I shall tell Their Lordships, perhaps you will kindly tell me what on earth persuaded you to do what you did.'

And Tommy told him.

THE END